Café Latte

18 UNUSUAL SHORT STORIES

Café Latte

18 UNUSUAL SHORT STORIES

Amit Shankar

Vitasta

Let Knowledge Spread

Published by
Renu Kaul Verma
For Vitasta Publishing Pvt Ltd
2/15 Ansari Road, Daryaganj,
New Delhi - 110 002
info@vitastapublishing.com

ISBN: 978-93-82711-44-5
© Amit Shankar 2014

Guest Editors: Shayantani Dutta Sen, Reshma Bhatnagar
Photo and Cover: Sarbajit Sarbajna
Layout: Vitasta Publishing Pvt Ltd
Printed at : Repro Knowledgecast Limited, Thane

I dedicate this title to Lord Shreenath Ji, who has blessed me with a new life, my father, Late Dr Vishnu, and to my darling sister, Manju Di, who fought so gallantly but eventually lost to Cancer.

The logic, if any

As a kid, there were always stories to describe things around me—moon to the sky, kings to the saints. This is how the world was introduced to me.

In-between high-pressure jobs, prolonged patches of quandary, during the past four years, I did manage to release three very distinctive titles; *Flight of the Hilsa, Chapter 11* and *Love is Vodka, A Shot Ain't Enough*. Considering my apathy towards brazen self-promotion, which now is a way of life with writers, all of them did reasonably well.

Raring to go ahead with my fourth title, I took a sabbatical again. The plot was formalized and chapter-wise break-up done. Some fifty-odd pages into the plot, during a visit to Agra, where I was supposed to attend a book reading session at the Agra Book Club, the twist happened.

"Why don't you attempt short stories?"

"They are so vain."

"But didn't you like them when you were a kid?"

"I did, but I can't write them."

"Have you ever tried?"

"But I can't."

"How do you know when you have not even tried?"

"What if I fail?"

"So what, you will still live to tell another story."

As a practice, I follow my heart. So here I am, with a very unusual compilation. Like my earlier work, this time also, I have just played the medium, typing the stories as they happened. I am confident you will like them. And if you do, my efforts would be rewarded.

Read them on a dark, gloomy day, with a hot cup of coffee or on a warm afternoon with a chilled can of beer. Turn the pages while looking out of your bay window or snuggle in bed with them, I assure you that the company would be truly worthwhile.

Please write in to share your views and reviews.

I can be reached at amitshankar73@gmail.com

Well, of course you can touch base with me on Facebook and Twitter too.

Facebook: https://www.facebook.com/Amitshankar.author

Twitter: amitshankar71

Website: www.amitshankar.in

Loads of love. Keep reading and keep smiling.

P.S. I have also included two stories of super-talented kids, Kartikey Sharma, and Vasundhara Goyal, aged ten and sixteen years respectively, whom I was fortunate to meet during a writing workshop.

Glad it is here

Why is a compilation of short stories written by an author called a 'collection'? Well, because the author dives into the recesses of his mind and finds figments of untold stories lying in disarray and 'collects' those wisps of ideas to pen down an aptly named 'collection'.

In his eclectic collection of unusual, short stories, Amit Shankar takes you on an engrossing journey. His stories are about humans rummaging in unusual pre-occupations, forging exceptional relationships, pursuing unconventional vocations and reacting unpredictably to situations thrust upon them. Whether it's the angst of the soul, a hint of the paranormal, the misery of ethos or the intuitiveness of the human spirit; he weaves a gripping tale, which unfolds like a screenplay, projecting itself on the silver screen of the reader's mind.

It could be easily said, with a degree of certainty, that this is one of his finest works so far and that he has successfully taken his craft of story-telling to a new level. Being a wordsmith, he reveals the required and conceals just the right amount, leaving something to the imagination and intellect of the reader. A couple of stories in this collection show immense promise to be developed into full-fledged novels or to be adapted as screenplays.

On a balmy evening, this is a book to be read in a shot, with black coffee and thoughtful musings. Trust me, this book has a sweet aftertaste!

— **Dr Shivani Chaturvedi**
Founder, Agra Book Club

Thank you

Neeraj Yadav for his valuable creative inputs and support.
Sarbajit aka Subzi for the beautiful cover design and communication support.
Shayantani Dutta Sen for her editorial support.
Reshma Bhatnagar for her editorial support.
Renu Kaul Verma for bringing the stories to you.
Veena Batra for her competent editing.
Megha Parmar for her marketing support.
Vagmi Kumar for all his encouragement.
Agra Book Club; a special word of thanks for inspiring me.

Contents

Temple Of The King

"*Dada*, what chord was that?" The disciple was in awe of the distinct sound of the infrequent guitar chord.

"You copy cat, first get your basics right." The master chuckled.

"Please *Dada*." The disciple pleaded.

"E Augmented seventh."

"Wow, that sounded so cool...had an explicit bluesy feel to it. Wish I could play like you."

"The day you stop copying me, you will."

"Do you really think so?" The disciple was still not sure.

"Put your heart into the melody and work on getting your own style. It is worth to be a bad original than a good copy." His fingers intricately strummed and deftly caressed the strings, producing an elaborate stringed symphony. The cigarette never left his lips.

Dada was everything a hero was supposed to be. Towering persona, imposing height, with apt diction, a glorious family history, award studded career and a benevolent heart. At six feet, his massive forearms could put any wrestler to shame. With Tagore's lineage, this product of Doon School, Dehradun, was a topper from JJ College of Arts, Mumbai and then a Gold Medalist from Parson's College, New York. Sabyasachi Tagore aka *Dada* was advertising's rock star. With more than five-dozen awards to his credit, he was more than what advertising could ever accommodate. No wonder, it had made him a recluse—a rolling stone.

"Ash, you have some stuff on you?"

"*Dada,* you have already rolled three since morning."

"You servicing shit bag, stop playing my mom." *Dada* was in no mood to be intimidated.

Ashish Monga aka Ash, was in the servicing team. But for some unknown reason, his motive for existence in advertising or even this world was *Dada*. He wanted to be like him—a free, independent, fearless soul, who lived to experiment, to seek, to fall and to learn. Ash was in awe of *Dada*'s character—his style, cocky attitude, intellect, the gift of the gab, articulation and complete annihilation of opponents, if any. Of all the things, Ash was also impressed with his grey hair, which he always referred to as the platinum crown! The only thing which Ash did not like was his aversion to family life. *Dada* led a bachelor's life, staying away from his family, if any. And this was the only topic *Dada* had never discussed with him.

It was not that Ash did not try. Once when he endeavored, *Dada* did not speak to him for months. Those were the most torturous times for Ash. He would pass by his cabin at least twenty times in a day, hoping to be called. On various pretenses he would walk up to him. *Dada* would just see through him. Lesson learnt. He knew that family topic was a taboo.

The December sun was pleasant, cutting through the freezing wind. *Dada* was in his usual attire—a leather jacket, faded denims and rider's boots. Ash being the servicing guy was in his business suit, tie and brogues. *Dada* always mocked the servicing team as a bunch of butlers. Knowing his volatile temper and immense physical strength, no one dared to refute him. Perched atop the railing, rolling his fourth joint, he looked at Ash.

"What have you planned for this New Year's Eve?"

"There is a campaign delivery on 1st of Jan."

"Are all servicing guys this dumb?" The snide remark had the right amount of sting. "I am asking about 31st, not 1st." He completed rolling the joint and lit it.

"What is the point of going anywhere and then returning the same night?" The traveller in Ash brooded. Travelling was a habit inculcated in him by *Dada*. Being an avid traveller himself, *Dada* coaxed him to go and see the world, experience it. Slowly Ash got hooked on to it.

"Dude, a moment of bliss is worth a lifetime of drudgery."

"Yeah, you are right, but then do you have anything specific?" Ash probed.

"You son of a gun, you are doubting my intellect?" He laughed and took a deep drag off the joint and passed it on to Ash.

Ash took a weighty puff and filled his lungs with the thick, milk like smoke. It curled up inside him, like a rattlesnake, dormant yet ready to kick in anytime.

"Let me take you to my dream destination." *Dada* looked intently towards the sky as if trying to find a fault with the formation of the clouds.

"Wow, that would be cool. And where would your dream place be? Venice?"

"You fuck brain moron, stop wasting your time watching these Bollywood craps. Venice is nothing but an overcrowded life on the sides of this pee like trickle which stinks as well. It has been promoted crazily and no wonder lapped up by the degenerated, second grade souls of this planet."

Ash loved *Dada*'s one sided and biased views. He totally doted on his unassuming part, which mostly took sides with the loser.

"Apologies, Your Highness, this mentally retarded, servicing shit bag pleads you to reveal your grand vision for the New Year's Eve." Ash smiled as he took another deep puff.

"Jagroi." He muttered and while he did, his eyes lit up.

"What? Where is that? Close to Kakori?" Ash sniggered.

"It is thirty five degrees south- east of Kasaul."

"*Dada*, please. Why can't you talk like a normal guy?" He beseeched.

"Because you mother fucker, as a traveller you are supposed to use the compass, direction of the sun and not GPS enabled phones or the Google map. God save your generation and this world." He took one last puff and stubbed the butt.

"*Dada*, please." Ash pleaded again.

"Well, it is somewhere near Tosh. We shall drive upto Kasaul, park the car there and trek for thirty kilometres south-east and should be there by noon."

"Sounds good. But never knew that some godforsaken place was your dream destination."

"As if you servicing mother fuckers are supposed to know anything. You jackass, now get back to work. We leave on 30th evening and we reach office on 1st morning. For us the champagne pops at Tosh."

*****

Armed with a steady supply of weed and scotch, they left. As a rule, Ash was supposed to drive whenever they went on a road trip. *Dada* preferred to roll on a stiff joint, put on some Iron Maiden, Floyd or Zepp and join them as a band member, doing his own air guitar and drum theatrics, while the music threatened to blast the roof of his Tata Safari.

The drive from Delhi to Kasaul was close to four hundred kilometers. Till Mandi, the landscape was quite monotonous. But as soon as they crossed it, everything changed; even the sky. Dotted with a million stars, it looked like an inverted saucer with million bulbs, or maybe holes showcasing the heavens beyond. Riding high on his white smoke train, by this time *Dada* had turned philosophical. He sat there, quietly, looking at the sky and the stars. His occasional deep breath and 'spectacular' were the only obvious movement and spoken word.

***

"You know Ash, if there was one wish this heartless God would ever grant me, I would ask him to let me die here, setting my soul free in these valleys." He sighed. "But then he won't, as he not only loves to control people and their lives, but also their souls."

"Come on *Dada*, you are going to live for another hundred years."

"Yeah and wet my bed with pee and poop. Sorry, not interested." His tone was unapologetic and curt.

"*Dada*, we are just hours away from the New Year's Eve,

let us talk of plans, dreams, journey, destination...."

"Don't ever talk of destination." He interrupted. "It's a farce." His voice was abrupt. "There is no destination before death." He looked at the sky, this time moving his fingers in the air as if arranging the stars. "Be the traveller that you are. Don't let the endpoint lure you or make you complacent and pretentious."

"But can one be a traveller all along?" The disciple's question was a valid one.

"What is this life if not a journey? Do you stop at one house, your first car, a pair of jeans, one CD, one watch, even one love? Son, to live life to its fullest, is all about being a traveller."

Ash seemed to be in coherence with *Dada's* viewpoint. Not that he had a choice, but his words made sense.

"*Dada* let us do something special today." Ash sounded high.

"Your special scares me." He flashed a childlike smile; innocuous.

"You always underestimate me. Let me get something for you. But before I leave, tell me why is this place your dream destination?"

Dada looked at the sky, making patterns with his fingers, in the air, as if rearranging the clouds in a better layout. He turned towards the hillock facing them.

"Can you see that small hill to my north-east side?"

"The one right in front of us?" Ash simplified his statement for better comprehension.

"No, the one to your north-east side." *Dada* reiterated himself.

"Yes, I can. Looks very scenic and serene."

"Ain't it perfect for having a quaint café? My café—The Traveller."

Ash was taken a little aback. He could not see any logic as to why a successful man like *Dada* would even think of having a café at such an abandoned spot. To him, *Dada* was more like a city man who loved his travel, but then also the pubs, the hot girls, the jazz evenings and the slick city life. And even if he could manage a café, who would come there? For a man who had seen the world, tasted the best that life had to offer, owning a desolate café was kind of a let down.

Maybe *Dada* read his string of thoughts. "I don't belong there." He pointed towards his back, the road that had got them there. "City life is a façade, devil's own way of consuming people, pulling them to the abyss and ensuring that they burn till eternity. Lust for power, money and position eats into us, leaving us like blabbering idiots, too blind to see the truth. I just want to have a café here, serve some Mexican coffee; nothing but the finest, and to make the traveller realize the little joys and surprises of travelling."

"Ok, now let me get something special for you." Ash started getting up.

Dada pulled him down, making him land back at the same spot.

"In a few minutes, the sun will go behind that café of mine. As it will cover my café, I want to watch that scene once with you. Learn, that it is not important to add anything to make the moment special. The trick lies in making every moment special by relishing it every second, by capturing it in your senses, by living it in its true splendid form and by being one with it."

Ash was too high to make much out of the long, reflective statement. Nevertheless, he nodded.

"Pass on my baby. Let me strum something for you." He ruffled his hair as Ash passed him his Fender—the twelve-string acoustic guitar.

"One day in the year of the fox
Came a time remembered well
When the strong young man of the rising sun
Heard the tolling of the great black bell

One day in the year of the fox
When the bell began to ring
Meant the time had cometh
For one to go
To the temple of the king

There in the middle of the circle he stands
Searching, seeking
With just one touch of his trembling hand

The answer will be found
Daylight waits while the old man sings

Heaven help me
And then like the rush of a thousand wings
It shines upon the one
And the day had just begun."

Whenever *Dada* sang his favorite; Temple of the King, Ash would get goose bumps. His smoke molested vocal chords with his ambidextrous hands on the guitar made him sound like a milder version of Bruce Springsteen.

The magic of his voice and guitar cast a spiritual gloom on every single being. An amount of stillness prevailed where everything was visible but only in the rear view mirror, on hindsight. Ash kept on rolling more and more joints, fuelling the spirit of *Dada*, his twelve-string baby and his soulful yearnings. As decided, they celebrated their New Year at his dream location, amidst weed, songs, sky and the stars.

***

The cardinal rule was followed on their way back too. Ash was driving and *Dada* was in the passenger's seat. The white rattlesnake had become a part of them, uniting with their minds and being. Their drive back to Delhi was a long one. Ash knew that his presence at the office was a must.

He forced his rattlesnake to snooze while he focused on the road ahead, still sinking the new philosophy within himself.

After driving for a few hours, he thought of stopping by. Some water would be fine, he told himself. As he got the water bottle, cranked the engine, he looked at *Dada*. He was blissfully unaware of everything, leaning against the side door of the car, comfortably numb.

As water gushed down Ash's throat, the parched passage took a sigh of relief. He gulped down at least three-fourth of the bottle.

"*Dada*, some water?"

He held the bottle for him.

"*Dada*, you have slept for long. Give this poor servicing shit bag some respite."

He still did not respond.

Ash shook him. No reaction. Instinctively he knew that something had gone haywire. He hit the brakes.

"*Dada*," he shook him with all this might.

Something was drastically wrong. He held *Dada*'s face and turned it towards him. It seemed that his neck had frozen, as it did not move even an inch. He used all his might and then the neck turned, like a gate on old rusted hinges.

In the side mirror, he could see *Dada* still looking at the sky, arranging the clouds.

***

Today Ash runs a small café, 'The Traveller' at Dada's dream destination. Every night, after shutting down, he strums *Dada's* guitar, sitting beside his grave singing his all-time favorite, Temple of the King.

After all, if life is a never-ending journey, the baton has to be passed on.

26 Down Express

"So you have come to receive someone?"

The basic premise of the question was idiotic. If at eight in the evening, someone was sitting at a deserted railway station, looking at his watch every few seconds, for sure the reason was obvious. But the question came from a man well into his sixties, to another in his early thirties, and therefore, was replied with caution.

"Yes." He responded with a distant smile.

"I see. Even I am here to receive someone. Someone very special." The smile from the confines of the crowfeet around his lips was non-apologetic.

The younger man smiled back again, as a sign of acknowledgement.

"My son is coming today." The utterance of the word

'son' made his face beam with paternal love and affection.

"That's nice." In his distant smile, the younger man tried feigning civility.

"His train has been delayed by an hour or so. You know how our Indian Railways is, never runs on time." He sounded a little disappointed. "What has this country come to? There was a time when trains were known by their arrival timing. Two 'o' clock local, Five thirty express, Seven thirty shuttle. If today we had the same trend, no train would get its name as they are never on time." The elderly man chuckled at his own joke, if there was any.

The younger man got up and walked towards the other end of the platform. His eyes scanned the dimly lit, deserted setting. A huge clock hung from what seemed like a few centuries old beam. Peeking through the dust, pigeon droppings and cobwebs, he could see that the glass was cracked and the hands were missing. The name of the station was a fading black paint on the yellow asbestos sheet, which was supported by cemented towers. The towers had small signage announcing the name of the station again. The four green benches bore testimony to the fact that the traffic at the station was minimal. Towards the far end of the station was the stationmaster's cabin. At the exit gate, there was a black board, on which the stationmaster used white chalk to update the train timings. A sleeping dog suddenly got up yelping as an urchin flung a stone at him near the exit gate.

The younger man watched the dog with distaste. What had he got himself into, he wondered. It had been a month since he had been posted to this sleepy little town, Ursala, which had recently got the status of SEZ. Suddenly big companies were elbow jostling for space, competing to establish their production facilities there. Being a small town, the station was a non-descript entity. Only four trains stopped there in the entire day with an average stoppage time of less than two minutes each.

"Sir, what is the position of 26 Down Express?" The younger man enquired.

"It has not reached the last station. Once it leaves Sealdah, I will get an update and will revise the same on the board." The stationmaster with the thick black-rimmed glasses mumbled.

"Thank you."

The younger man ambled towards the shed. At least it had some light. The rest of the station looked spooky. He was getting a little irritated. He had asked his wife to take the morning train so that he could receive her around noon. Being pally with his supervisor, taking a half-day off was not tough for him. But then like any other woman, his wife insisted on doing what she was told not to.

"What is he saying?" The old man's voice was scratchy – maybe it was age, or maybe impatience.

The younger man could not hear him clearly. Reluctantly,

he walked towards him.

"What did he say?" He adjusted his specs, getting the younger man in focus.

"Who?"

"Who else but the stationmaster."

"Oh, he said that he has no update as of now." The younger man sat down.

"Useless guy." He smirked, "I have been seeing him for all these years. Some people are plain stupid."

He was a man in his early sixties. His silver white hair was kept slightly long for a man his age. Wearing a brown shirt and black trousers, his feet were encased in tan sandals. The pocket of his shirt had a spectacles case and a fountain pen.

"Son, what is your name?

The younger man looked at him.

"I hope you don't mind me addressing you as son. You are as young as him." He smiled fondly.

"I am Bikash."

"Vikas?"

"No, it is Bikash, as in *kaash*." The younger man tried explaining the correct pronunciation.

"Ah, a Bengali. Aren't you? Only they would pronounce Vikas as Bikash. It's that same *Bidda Balan* thing." He chuckled at his wit again. "I am Sooraj, Sooraj Gupta—a *baniya*. You know, the people who live and die for money." This time his chuckle was replaced with a guffaw.

As he laughed, a nasty spell of cough hit him. Bikash looked at him, waiting for the cough to subside on its own. But it just kept on aggravating. His raspy laughter turned into gasps. The stillness of the platform started echoing with his loud, unruly and uncontrollable cough. The dog started wailing somewhere in the background as if disturbed by the sudden human cacophony. Bikash got up and started patting his back. Gradually, the intensity of the cough started to subside.

"Thank you, son." He opened his bag and pulled out a small water bottle and took a sip from it. "See, I addressed you as a son and you acted like one." He smiled. The strenuous coughing had made his face turn red. For the first time Bikash noticed that he had a very soft and kind face.

"So who is coming?"

"My wife." Bikash grinned.

"Where is she coming from?"

"Her mom's place."

"Nice."

"Who else is there?"

"Where?"

"I mean here, in your family."

"Oh, my daughter."

"She is lucky to have a father like you."

Bikash smiled, accepting his compliment gracefully.

"What is her name?"

"Tinni."

"Ah, sweet name." His lips moved as he said the name silently to himself.

Bikash glanced at his watch. Four minutes past nine. He gazed towards the end of the platform, hoping the signal to be green, which would mean that the train was approaching. But the signal was still red.

Suddenly Mr Gupta blurted out. "You take good care of Tinni. She is a sweet girl."

Bikash's eyes had a quizzical look while he stared at Mr Gupta. The old man was staring vacantly at the hot and humid air.

"I did not get you." His tone of surprise was genuine.

Mr Gupta had an urgent edge in his voice, as he caught his arm. "Bikash, give her whatever she needs. She is a sweet child. You are all that she has. Give her all that she deserves and wants. Tinni is a very special child. You have to take extra care of her. She would need you and all your attention. Don't worry, it is going to be alright."

"What nonsense is this?" Bikash jerked off his hand and got up from the bench. His face was a mix of disgust and bewilderment.

"I mean it. She is a very sweet child. Oh God, why are you so cruel?" Mr Gupta was in some kind of trance, murmuring incoherently and shaking his head vehemently.

"Please stop. Please." Bikash bellowed. Mr Gupta was

still in a state of daze, his eyes clouded and face pale.

"Just because I'm respecting your age and having a conversation, it gives you no right to get personal. Who the hell are you to tell me what I should do for my daughter?" Bikash was infuriated.

"No, no, you are getting me wrong. I did not mean to upset you. I just felt the urge of saying it. Don't know why, but I just felt the urge, so I did. Apologies if I offended you." The old man suddenly seemed to take control of his outburst. He wiped his brows very quietly, slouched his shoulders, as if trying to disappear within himself.

Unexpectedly, there was a distant sound of a train's whistle. It punctuated both; the apology and the anger. Bikash and Mr Gupta looked towards the side from which 26 Down was expected. But the signal was still red. Bikash looked towards the other side. The signal was green and he could see the potent headlights of a train cutting through the darkness. Dejected, he sat on the bench again. Suddenly, Mr Gupta started sprinting towards the approaching train in a spurt of energy. Bikash was too shocked to react. But impulsively, he wanted to stop him. Even after all that had transpired between them, he could not stop himself.

"Anjan, Anjan, Anjan, where are you, where are you, son?" Like a man possessed, Mr Gupta was dashing towards the approaching train.

Damn, was this old man going to commit suicide? The

thought spooked Bikash.

"Gupta *ji,* stop. Please stop Gupta *ji.*" Bikash ran after him.

The train was getting closer. He put in all his energy, trying to catch up with him. But the old man, despite his age, seemed to have developed wings on his feet. The train was coursing through the platform.

"Anjan, where are you, son, tell me, where are you?"

Mr Gupta was still screaming something and by now had gained a considerable distance.

"Gupta *ji,* stop. Please Gupta *ji.*" Bikash screamed again. He realized that his screams and requests were getting drowned in the rumble of the chugging engine and iron wheels.

Mr Gupta, not paying any attention, was running frightfully close to the approaching headlights.

"Gupta *ji,* please stop. It is not safe." Bikash was still running after him, on the platform. The few neon lights were left far behind. He strained his eyes to see that the train missed Mr Gupta by inches and hurled down the track. In time, he pulled himself back, away from the momentum of the passing train. Out of breath, he could see Gupta *ji* still running in the opposite direction, towards the end of the platform.

Using the sleeve of his shirt, he wiped his face. When he looked towards the direction of Mr Gupta, he was nowhere in sight. He looked around, searching for some trace of him.

The stationmaster was walking back towards his cabin. The train had passed. The platform was suddenly very quiet. The whistle of the train was getting feeble. The mongrel sat still as if very surprised to see so much of activity.

"Gupta *ji,* you there?" Bikash looked around wondering where could he disappear. Did he fall on the line? He shuddered at the thought. But then it was important to assuage his fears. He walked towards the track, and looked intently. It was dark. He could see the gleaming metal rail. As far as his eyes could see, there was no sign of Mr Gupta's body. Where did he disappear, he thought to himself.

Still out of breath, he cursed his sedentary life style and promised himself that he would start going for regular evening walks. Confused, he walked towards the bench, planning to catch his breath. He sat there looking towards the red signal.

Twenty- five minutes past nine, his watch declared.

"What happened? All well?"

The sudden voice made him turn.

The stationmaster was standing there, still holding the lantern.

"Yes, I am fine. Just that there was this elderly gentleman, who suddenly started running towards the train."

"You mean the guy with white hair and specs?"

"Yes, Gupta *ji.*" Bikash confirmed.

"Don't you worry. He has been coming here for years. He is not mentally stable. Bloody lunatic."

"Oh." Bikash felt a surge of sympathy towards Mr Gupta.

"But he did not come across as unstable or a lunatic. You know what I mean."

The stationmaster laughed. "Yeah, he is saner of the lot. Three years back, his son was supposed to come. He never came and his father, the man you met, got no news of him. Since that day, he has been coming here daily at this hour chasing every train, shouting his son's name."

"Oh, that is very unfortunate. God is cruel at times."

"What was he talking about?" The stationmaster sat down next to Bikash.

"Nothing, general chit-chat."

"I see."

Something urged Bikash to share his brief interaction with the stationmaster. "He was talking normally, but then suddenly he got a little hysterical and started talking about my daughter."

Fear circulated the stationmaster's face, which he did try to conceal. But it was so evident in his eyes that it made Bikash uneasy.

"What happened?"

"Nothing." The stationmaster feigned innocence.

"He started telling me that I have to take care of her,

treat her well. Damn, she is my daughter; of course I have to take care of her." For some reason, Bikash could not help but share the entire episode.

The stationmaster got uneasy and shifted on the bench. He looked at Bikash.

"Now that you have mentioned it, I can recall few other people stating the same."

"What?" The awkward feeling mounted.

"Nothing. You know how locals talk."

"Why, what do they say?

"Well, they say that he is some kind of a messenger who delivers messages from the higher-ups."

Bikash looked confused.

"The pain in his life has made him align with certain paranormal forces, enabling him to connect with messages that have been undelivered. He becomes the messenger for these forces, the dead ones, delivering messages on their behalf."

"Is this some kind of a joke?" Bikash could not control his fear mixed with anger.

"Don't get worked up. I already told you that all this is nothing but the blabber of the locals."

The stationmaster got up and started walking towards his cabin. Suddenly he stopped.

"You had come enquiring about the 26 Down?"

"Yes."

"It won't be in for another two hours or so."

"Why?"

"There has been a case of attempt to robbery and death."

"What?" Bikash was stunned.

"Yes, Some burglar tried snatching a purse from a woman on 26 Down, when it started from the previous station. The woman resisted and in the scuffle, she fell down from the compartment door on the train track and died. So the train has been stopped there. It will take at least two hours more."

"When did this happen?" Bikash was afraid to ask the question.

"Around nine. Why?" The stationmaster asked out of sheer curiosity.

A solitary bead of cold sweat trickled down Bikash's neck. He now recollected that around the same time Gupta *ji* had suddenly got hysterical, telling him to take care of his daughter. Was the lady on the train his wife? Did she choose the senile old man—Gupta *ji* to deliver her last desperate message to him?

ଔ❖ഇ

Code Of Honor

Dear Raghav,

What does it take to be a man?

Balls and that too of steel.

I write to you, sitting in my bunker, stealing glances at my mission, my victory and the ultimate destination—Manu Peak. This daunting peak will prove whether I have the balls made of steel or not. After all, every pursuit is aimed towards proving a point to our own selves.

Yesterday evening was a very special day. For the past few days we were on a high alert. We knew that we were waiting for orders from the central command. An order was all that could have given me and every single soldier of my unit what we live for—pride and glory. Finally, my CO *Sahib* called me and instructed to mount an offensive on the Manu Peak, with five other *jawaans*.

This mission will be the toughest one as we are supposed to engage the enemy from the rear side so that the rest of the platoon can mount an offensive from the front. You know Raghav, I have lived for this moment all my life, when I can finally do something, which will make my life worthwhile. I might be sounding selfish, but this is my moment of glory and I will claim it.

Remember, you used to laugh at my moustache? I know, you were embarrassed to see your father in a thick, twirled moustache. I also agree, that in normal city life, it does seem to be a little odd. But do you know the real reason behind it? There are two.

First, every moment, every day, amidst all this chaos, degradation of morals, character, this moustache was my reality check. It made me realize that the epitome of manhood I carried so proudly on my face, came with a huge responsibility. I guess I have never done anything that would have let my moustache down. It was my way of wearing my valor, my commitment to my country and my loyalty. Every time, I would be tempted to do anything meant for lesser mortals, I would get petrified of facing myself in the mirror the next day, with my thick moustache.

The second reason; and I'm not trying to prove anything to you, the government gives a moustache allowance. Nothing major; around five hundred rupees a month. I have been saving this money for you, for all these years. The last time I was there with you, I remember you wanted a bike. This time we will go together and get a bike for you. I hope you will get a good one for fifty thousand. Now that I think of it, I would love to ride with you, on your new bike, feeling the wind in my moustache. Would you take me along?

Raghav, I know as a father I have not been able to live up to your expectation. It is not that I am gifting you the bike to make up for the same or that I did not try being a good father. I did. But then maybe our points of view differed. I'm sure that you know that my father left me with nothing. After completing my school from our ancestral village, due to lack of choices, I enrolled in the army. Back then, joining the army had more to do with a feeling of social security than upholding the country's pride. As a *jawaan*, I was entitled to accommodation, food and uniform. This was more than what I needed. Then I got married. This was again not a choice, which I made. Your mother never asked for anything; I mean not even a *saree*. Her simplicity made me realize that I was responsible towards her, for her needs, and her happiness. And then you happened. You were my choice. I wanted someone to call me Papa. When I held you in my hands for the first time, at the Army Hospital, Jamnagar, I could not help but adore everything about you. You were so tiny that you fitted in my palms. You were so tender that I was afraid that my rough hands would hurt you. I still remember your mother lying on the bed, with nurse standing there, in front of me, and you in my hands. I was so lost in you that I could not even hear the nurse who was asking me to hand you back to her.

Just that one moment and I knew that I would do whatever it took to give you the power to make choices.

Shelling is increasing. The Pakistanis fire a shell after every three to four minutes. If you were here, you would have covered your ears. The sound of a shell is deafening. When I was young, I used to cringe with fear everytime a shell was fired. But now I guess I have accepted it as a part of my existence.

I know I have never written you long letters. But then there is always a new day. Raghav, I would have spoken to everyone I could have thought of, regarding you, your future and the way ahead. Everyone told me that being in the army was the safest bet to rear you the way I wanted to. Maybe I was too naïve to have taken their advice, maybe I did the right thing, maybe I didn't. In hindsight, dissecting choices becomes easy. Your mother has told me that during your formative years, during every Parent-Teacher meeting you used to ask why I wasn't there like other fathers. You had a reason, a valid one. I know that there were times when I was not present to celebrate your birthdays too, to hold your hands while you cut your birthday cake. You had every reason to be upset. But then it was not that I did not want to. It was the circumstances that never let me. I had to be away, so that I could put that fancy cake on your table.

I wanted to give you the best. And for you to have it, money was needed. For a soldier, his means are limited. And being a soldier was the only life I knew of. I shudder at the thought of being a civilian, living, eating and thinking like one. No wonder, to give you the best, I had to take forward posting to non-family stations. This doubled my salary.

Though we can endlessly debate on this subject, but then sleeping in bunkers, tents, facing the hostile environment, living under constant threat was a choice made by me, so that I was able to give you a better life.

You know Raghav, I really wanted you to join the army. In a couple of months, you will be joining college. We have had this discussion many a times and I know that the olive green does not fascinate you. Is it because it reminds you of your father who was never there for you? If that were the case, I would urge you to reconsider your decision. This is the only career that makes you a man, lets you be one for as long as you want and gives you an opportunity to live by a code of honor and then die by it. Pride and honor for the country, our army, our unit is the only driving force. I know of people in my village, who opened up shops, got into small businesses. They all are making good money, at least more than me. But then I have my doubts if they are lucky to have a reason to live and die for.

You are a bright boy, you will do well in life; maybe as discussed with me, will go for an MBA, join some multi-national, earn loads of money, drive big cars, travel abroad. On the other hand, what would the army give you? Not the hefty pay cheque and the perks, but it would let you be the man that you are, every moment. The shining buckle of your belt, the lion on your cap, the story behind every medal, being looked upon as a hero by people around you is something to die for. A death, which is reserved only for the heroes. Wrapped in tri-color flag as twenty-one guns fire, you feel like getting up once again to salute the sense of valor. Glory at its best, making death more glamorous than a million lives. At least, this is the death I seek for myself.

I know every child is a father of a man. The day this child, who would be a father soon, can ensure that he would be a man in the true sense of the word, he would produce another man. Raghav, are you getting me? Hope you don't fold this letter, like the earlier ones, and stash it away in your trunk, leaving my words for the termites. I don't think they will understand the whole concept of pride and honor, as they are not meant to.

A shell has just landed around a hundred metres away from my bunker. It was a loud explosion. *Saale* Pakistani, just few hours more and they will have to pay for every bullet, every shell, with their lives. You know son, I know this is a suicide mission. But for my unit, my men, my country, I have to claim the peak. Someone has to, and I am proud that I have been blessed with this opportunity. While I drive my bayonet up their guts, I want *"Bharat mata ki jai"* to be the last word they would ever hear. I am a soldier and I respect another soldier. Therefore I want to give them the honor of dying for their country. I hope in turn, I get the same.

I know there is a generation gap between you and me. I don't understand your world of Internet, sms, chat, Facebook and other nuances. Not that I don't know of these upgrades, but then to me they look so vain. Why would anyone want the world to know where he had his lunch, which movie he went to, what is he wearing, what he thinks of others? But let me not tread that path, as I can see you getting upset. I like Facebook, I mean it. Remember when we had gone to Jammu and you had posted your picture with your mother and I, your friends went gaga over my moustache? I quite liked the fact that younger people liked it. Have you ever thought of keeping a moustache like me? I know you hate even a pencil line there but as I write this, I'm trying to visualize you with a thick, twirled up moustache. Trust me, it will suit you.

Today, as I write to you, I feel so much at ease. I think I have done my bit for you by saving enough to ensure a decent education, a decent life for you and your mother, shielding you from all the harshness that this world has to offer.

Wish I had shared all this with you earlier. Maybe, it would have made us a better father–son duo, a better family. Anyways, better late than never. I have lived like a soldier, a father, a husband, a son, a friend; discharging all my duties. Now, the time has come to claim my highest honor; which is reserved only for a soldier—dying for my country, claiming my honor, and justifying my pride of all these years. Someday, you will understand this.

Once I am gone, I don't want you to cry or feel bitter about the whole thing. This is a choice I have made and I am proud of it. I know you will never join the forces. But that is ok. We all have to live by our code of honor, which we choose ourselves. Can I make a small request? When you get the petrol pump or the gas agency allotted, please ensure that you run it with all honesty. For making a few extra rupees, don't malign my name and give any chance to people to scoff at my moustache.

Take care of you mother. You are blessed to have her in your life. If you had a bad father….

The last few paragraphs were washed away as ink could not withstand the deluge of tears.

***

Today, Captain RaghavYadav is a proud soldier. Every time he twirls his moustache; which is getting thicker by the day, he is reminded of the fact that to live is all about pride, and to die, nothing but honor.

ର❖ଛ

The Jazz Player

Perfect and shining, he mused as he looked at them. He was happy to see the result of his effort. After all, the entire last hour or so was spent polishing them. Though a little worn out, but after a nice coat of wax, they looked perfect. On to the right side, on the wall, on a wooden hanger, a black suit awaited, with a red tie and a white shirt. The small cardboard box lying on the bed had his gig hat. Today was a big day for him. He had been living for this day for too long.

He got up from the chair and walked towards the wall. It had the only door to his one room apartment. He opened the door and looked outside. The lane was buzzing with everyday activity and commotion. Today, instead of cursing the noise and the crowd, he smiled at the ignorance of the world outside. They had no clue how special this day was, he thought to himself and closed the door.

Standing in front of a small circular mirror, he checked his face. The deep creases on his cheeks and forehead accentuated his charm. For someone who had witnessed seventy-six springs, he looked good. His white, closely trimmed moustache added that perfect contrast to the deep tan on his skin inherited from God's own country; Kerala. Though he had shaved early in the morning, he could again feel some roughness on his face. Immediately, the shaving brush was put to task—whipping up lather in the shaving soap container. The Topaz shaving blade was flipped sides in the razor to give him that real close shave.

He came out of his shaving adventure to the small, stuffed and crowded twelve by ten room. The corner next to the green window was kept absolutely spic and span. It seemed as if that area had been sterilized for a higher purpose; maybe to accommodate a table with a picture of Christ or maybe some other reason. He walked to the makeshift kitchen and opened a small plastic box. His fingers fiddled inside, as if searching for something, till they found it; a measuring tape. Using that worn out tape, he measured the corner space repeatedly, measuring its width, height and depth. Punctuating the measuring spree at times, he would himself stand in the corner for a correct assessment.

***

Dressed in his black suit, which now hung loosely over his shrinking body, the well-laundered white shirt, red tie and the worn out black hat with silk band, Julias Sebastian hurried his way through the lanes of Jawahar Park, carrying a battered case which held the joy of his life; his saxophone. Being an unauthorized colony, it doubtlessly looked like one—lack of proper streets, lights, sanitation or any planning.

For all these years, fighting his existence in relative penury and living for the love of Jazz, he could never make any physical assets. When he was young, in his twenties, he was too smitten by the creative brilliance of Swing Jazz and Cool Jazz. With Miles Davis as his God, all he wanted to be was a Jazz Musician. His parents worked as house helpers to an aristocrat British couple. It was here; in the Luyten's Delhi Bungalow that he heard the 'black plate' play music on a gramophone. So smitten was he, that whenever the *'Gora Sahib'* played the record, he would press his ears to the wall, to soak his soul in the seductive melody of Jazz. When he was ten or maybe twelve years old, India got its independence. The *Gora Sahib* had to leave. Before he did, he gifted the gramophone and all his records to the little lover of Jazz, Julias Sebastian.

At fifteen, Julias picked up the saxophone and the affair of his lifetime started. In and out of relationships, finally he accepted that maybe the divine wanted him to serve Jazz. In

Independent India, flourishing India, the Jazz music scene was restricted largely to five star hotels. His gigs remunerated him well and playing at a hotel meant free food and imported liquor too. But then, the music scene changed and Disco took over.

Prolonged playing of the saxophone and excessive smoking had given him a condition called *Zenker's Diverticulum*. It was a condition of the larynx, which inflamed the vocal chords. His doctor had asked him to cut down on both the loves of his life; smoking and playing the saxophone.

With lesser gigs and old age health hassles, survival was getting tougher. For the past ten years, he had been putting up at Jawahar Park. His modest dwelling and paper-thin earnings barely kept him above the poverty line. There were times when he wanted to end it all. But then being a Catholic, that right was also with the divine. From three-course meals, he had to move to two and now they were restricted to one. He never wanted or aspired for anything, except playing Jazz. But like every other mortal he too had a fantasy, albeit one with a difference.

***

"Good afternoon."

"How come you are all dressed up and that too so early? Hope not getting married?" The shopkeeper laughed.

Julias' dark, wrinkled face turned purple with a deep

blush. "Stop kidding, Mat. Maybe you will get to attend my wedding in your next life. Keep your tuxedo ready to be the best man." They both laughed.

"I hope she is still there." Julias asked in a low tone, his eyes sparkling.

"You crazy old man, I swear." Mat was exasperated.

"Why crazy? Can't I have my little pleasures?"

"But Julias, this is not right."

"Why? Am I doing something immoral, is it some kind of a sin?"

"But, what would people say? I mean it is outright shocking. I have never seen anyone come to me with this request."

"Let us not go there."

"I am your friend."

"So act like one. There is a price to what I want. I know I can't afford her, but then I have saved for all these years, just to have her."

"You are crazy." Mat shrugged his shoulders.

"Well, I don't care", Julias was adamant.

"People will make fun of you."

"Their pokes can't be more cruel than life's own and what I have been getting for all these years."

"Are you sure that you want to do this?"

"Never felt more convinced."

"You crazy son of a life."

They both laughed.

"Listen," Julias pulled out a wad of notes, tied with rubber band. "This is sixty. The balance eight thousand, post I see her at my place."

"It seems you have hit the Jackpot."

"No, not really. Have got a gig at the Embassy of Norway. They are paying me twenty-five thousand. So I thought of having her first. Every man has a right to his kinks, doesn't he?

Mat just shrugged his shoulders again.

"Here are the keys. You know where my place is. Right? Please send her around six. I would have taken her myself but you know how people there are. I don't want to end up being a laughing stock. I will get back to her as soon as I get free." Excitement was written all over Julias' face.

He got up and looked at the surprised face of his friend, Mat. "And dress her up in blue silk. I love the feel of soft silk."

***

Though it was February, the afternoon sun was hot. The Embassy of Norway was celebrating Independence Day. The front lawn of the Embassy was inundated with people; all rich and powerful. Ambassadors to bureaucrats, politicians to socialites, of course, the media too.

In a corner, under a quaint tree, on a small podium stood Julias Sebastian, with a mike attached to his saxophone, straining his vocal chords and playing "Morbid Town", one of his favorite Jazz compositions. The crowd was not even bothered about his existence or music. He was just there to create some ambient interlude to support the ongoing conversations or to create the perfect film scene. Initially, when he had started out, this approach towards Jazz infuriated him. But over the long years, he had accepted that Jazz in India could only serve as a background score to chit chat and conversation.

Julias shunned the negative thoughts from his mind. Today was a big day for him. He had to be smiling, in high spirits. His performance was scheduled for two hours. Five minutes into his first set, he felt his neck choke. He was not finding enough air in his lungs to blow the demanding passage of the saxophone. He took a break and signaled one of the many gloved waiters. The red wine helped to douse what seemed like a bagful of sand in his throat.

When he had agreed to do this gig, he knew that playing a hundred- minute set would be impossible for him. But greed pushed him. Also, the event manager had no choice, as there were hardly any Jazz saxophone players in and around Delhi. Julias knew that he had to complete his set, take the money and walk out, to the love of his life—the blue silk waiting at his place.

He decided to play the easier numbers, as they would strain his vocal chords a little less. The crowd wouldn't even know of it. But in no time he was faced by the Jazz player in him, berating and castigating his attitude towards music and his diminishing love for Jazz. He got back to playing the tougher numbers, at the cost of his lungs and vocal chords.

***

With twenty-five thousand in his pocket, a wine bottle and five thousand rupees as a gift from the Embassy, Julias' energy was at an all time high. He was feeling like a sixteen-year-old, going to meet his beloved for the very first time. It was nearly six in the evening and he knew that his fantasy would have been delivered. A fantasy that had consumed all his savings. But then he had no one to save for. He cursed himself for not having a mobile phone. He knew that probably only two people in the entire country did not have one; Jesus and Julias. If he had one, he could have called to confirm the arrival of blue silk. Gosh, he was dying to see her there, in his apartment. After so many years, he could feel the adrenaline rush. He felt so alive, so much in tune with the vibes of the world. He felt so good, after so long.

He could see auto rickshaws parked at the other side of the road. Though he commuted using metro or bus, today being a special day he was entitled to some perks. His veins were throbbing, his heart pounding and his throat was getting parched. He just wanted to run and be there. The time lapse was killing him. Balancing the wine bottle, the sax case and the bouquet, he crossed the street.

***

"*Janaab*, it is a hit and run case. The deceased is a seventy-year-old man. Most probably a musician. He was carrying a flute like instrument. I think he was drunk, as alcohol was found on him along with a broken bottle of wine. Yes *janaab*, sending his body for postmortem. No phone found either."

***

"*Janaab*, it has been seven days. The postmortem report has also come. During the time of accident, he was drunk and was crossing Shanti Path when a speeding car hit him. We have done the preliminary enquiry too. A couple of auto rickshaw drivers have seen the accident happen. No one could remember the number of the speeding car. We have taken their statements. The deceased had no identity, nothing on him; just a flute. No *janaab*, no wallet, no money. We have placed an advertisement in the local newspaper too. No response. No relative has come forward to claim the body. Guess we should put the body under unclaimed and do the last rites at an electric crematorium."

***

In a one-room apartment at Jawahar Park, amidst all the clutter and chaos, in a tidy corner stood a coffin, vertically. With intricate carving of angels, its floral marble inlay work on the sides, the shining brass hinges and clasps, it was fit to hold a king. The inner casket, which was lined with blue silk, had a small note pasted.

"Dear Julias, it is odd for a living man to buy his own coffin. But then you have always been the odd one. This coffin will fulfill your desire to be buried as a king. Going out of town, to Kerala, for twenty-one days. Keep my balance ready. Will come to collect once I'm back. Mat"

P.S. Hope the coffin doesn't tempt you to die early.

Let Me Help You Die

"Good morning, sister." Doctor Prakash walked into his clinic. It was nine am and he was dressed to address the day. In his immaculately ironed navy blue suit, pink shirt, black shoes with matching belt and tie, he looked the perfect, suave doctor.

"Good morning, Sir, your favorite patient is back." The nurse smiled as she took the files from Dr Prakash, who did not get her sarcasm.

"Who?"

"Pankaj Saxena. He was brought in here yesterday night. He had consumed rat poison."

"What? Again?" Dr Prakash took off his coat and handed it over to the nurse.

"Yes, Sir. If we count this time, it is his fourth visit."

She placed some reports and files on the table in front of the doctor.

"How is he doing?"

"Out of danger. We pumped his stomach, washed it and have put him on drip. He is stable. I have kept the test reports on your table."

"I will see him during my rounds." Dr Prakash skimmed through the papers at his desk, lost in thoughts and visibly upset.

***

"So you are back?" Dr Prakash was examining his reports.

"Good morning, doctor. I am so glad to see you. Yesterday night I told them to call you. I knew that if you were there, I wouldn't die." Pankaj mumbled. He was looking weak, washed out and still in a delirious state. Maybe the medicines wanted him to stay that way.

"Pankaj, why do you keep doing this?" The impatient edge in the doctor's voice was obvious.

"Doc, life is a bitch. How can I help it?" He slurred.

"Don't be melodramatic. You are just stupid. I have prescribed some drugs. Before you are discharged, come and see me."

"Doctor, please…"

"You need rest. Don't strain yourself. You have lost lot

of fluid. See me before you leave."

Dr Prakash sauntered away.

***

"What is your problem?

"Too many. Doc, my life is full of them. From where should I start?"

"Pankaj, I am not your counsellor, understand? I just want to warn you that now it is getting too much."

"What?"

"Your act, this pretense of dying, disinterest in living. It's all rubbish." Dr Prakash was angry. "Please stop it now."

"You think I am doing all this to gain sympathy?"

"I'm certain."

"Doc, you are being insensitive."

"And you are being stupid. One day you will repeat this silly act again and it will be too late."

"But I want to die. I really do. Let my beloved named death, carry me in a chariot made of white light and feathers." Pankaj looked up, as if imagining the lines he was narrating.

"Look, Pankaj, I appreciate your poetic romance and all that. But please understand that as doctors we spend years perfecting the science of saving a life. We put in our every bit in knowing and learning more about this body, so that during the times of emergency, we can be the life savers.

When someone commits suicide, it is like an insult to our years of hard work. It is like a tight slap on our faces. Life is precious; it is not to be thrown away."

"Doc, I do appreciate this sermon coming from you. But at my end, life sucks and death is the only solution."

"Pankaj, no one wants to die. If anyone gets a second chance, he will never repeat the mistake of committing suicide."

"You have your facts misplaced." Pankaj challenged.

"So what is the truth, Pankaj?"

"I want to die. Don't know why this bitch called life is not letting me." The smirk on his face was mocking the doctor and his whole value system.

"You really want to die?"

"Yes, I do."

"Pankaj, think before you speak. Do you really want to die?"

"Yes, yes, I want to." The nodding was vehement.

"Ok. I saved your life four times. But you failed to see my value and appreciate my efforts. If I help you in dying, maybe you will appreciate me more."

"What?"

"Pankaj, I will help you in dying."

"Are you out of your mind?" He was clearly taken aback by the preposterous offer.

"No, we are talking business." The doctor smiled.

"I will visit your place this Sunday at four pm. Be ready to die. I assure you there will be no vomit, no loosened sphincter, no mess, just luxurious and easy death, sure shot."

"Doc, you can't be serious?"

"But you just said that you seriously want to die. I am taking the same seriousness and expanding upon it." The doctor smiled, a smile, which had the challenge-accepting streak.

"Yes, but…"

"I will be there at 4 pm sharp. Be ready."

***

"Hi Doc." The voice at the other end of the line was shaky.

"All well?" The doctor smiled.

"Yes sure, I just wanted to confirm that you were kidding that day, right?"

"You mean about helping you die?"

"Yes."

"Pankaj, am I your *jija*, your friend, or a clown that I would fool around with you?"

"But how can you kill someone?" The tonal quality was getting shriller.

"Because that is what you want. Don't you?"

"Yes." He stammered.

"So what is the problem? I am helping you achieve your dream journey. You should be thankful to me." The playful tone was getting warmer as the doctor had started enjoying the game.

"But don't you think it is wrong?"

"What, helping a patient die? Only the two of us would know this secret. The first one, you, won't be able to tell and the other one, that would be me. So what is the hassle?"

"Nothing. I am not afraid of dying." The defiant note in Pankaj's voice was rising, yet unsure.

"That is the spirit. Enjoy life for the coming three days. I will be there on Sunday, 4 pm."

***

"Hi Doc." His voice was groggy with sleep. He had scrambled up to receive the call.

"Hey there. How are you, young man? All set for the big day? Just two more days to go."

"Doc, you really think this is going to work out?"

"Pankaj, if you are scared and if you don't want to die, I can't force you. I helped you getting back your life on more than one occasion. But you showed no gratitude and turned into a habitual offender, throwing your life at your own will. Remember, when we had the last conversation at my clinic, I did ask you to stop all this. But you insisted that you truly want to die. So as your friend I thought of giving you what you wanted, a sure shot death. And who better than me, a doctor, to ensure the same?"

"But you see..." the sleepy voice was now awake and deliberate.

"What? Not sure if you want to die?"

"No, no, I want to. But you know ..."

"Say it Pankaj, it is your life. I can't force you. If you love your life, choose it over death."

"Can I call you back?" The request was shaky.

"Please feel free. I shall be waiting. By the way, just to let you know, I have chosen four ways for you. All of them safe, painless and sure. Bye, have a good day."

***

"Hi Pankaj. You were not answering my calls. So as per the prior appointment, I thought of visiting you. Hope you are not busy?"

Pankaj was in a state of shock the moment he saw Dr Prakash standing at his doorstep. Had he known that he would actually show up, he would have never answered the door.

"Can I come in?" The doctor requested.

"Yeah, sure, please do." He moved to one side, making way for the doctor. A two-room apartment was all he had and it was grossly unkempt and nearly in shambles. The living room just had a couch, a dust coated side table, which had a telephone and a 32-inch TV mounted on the wall. The dining table was nothing but a platform to keep objects. From beer bottles to paper cups, cartons of food to bills, everything was stacked on it. The dining chairs were replaced with three stools.

The doctor moved towards the adjoining room. It had a double bed that was acting as a dumping ground for clothes. The stench of stale food, liquor and cigarettes was nauseating. He saw the pizza box strewn under the bed accompanied by an upturned coke can. His disgusted face shook involuntarily from side to side and he decided against visiting the second room.

He pulled a stool and placed it close to Pankaj.

"Even now you can say that suicide for you was just an act to get sympathy." The doctor gave him one more chance to succumb to his fears, "you never wanted to die as you were scared of death like any other man."

But some people never learn. "Death is my beloved. Show me a man who has been afraid of a beloved as beautiful as her?"

"Wow, I love your idea of romancing death. I always knew that you were not one among the crowd. That is why, as per my promise, I have got four options for you."

The doctor opened his bag and pulled out four packets. Like a magician, with great dexterity, he placed the four packets on the other stool. Pankaj was watching with horror, shock and fear in his eyes. The romance was gone.

The doctor looked up, trying to lock his eyes with Pankaj's. Pankaj was hesitant to do so. He was staring at the packets on the stool.

"Today is going to be your last day. Why don't we make it interesting?"

"I did not get you."

"Let us play a game. I want you to die like a real hero, a lover, who is leaving this world with his beloved named Death. Sounds romantic? I bet it does to you. Ok, we will play this game called *Kaun Banega Crorepati*."

Pankaj started wiping his clammy palms on his short sleeves. The doctor did not pay attention to his confused condition.

"What happened?"

"You are crazy, doctor. I swear you are."

"Why do you think so? I am just a normal man, your friend, who is trying to help a romantic man meet his beloved. I wish I had the balls to be as crazy as you. I mean four suicide attempts and even then God decided not to take you. Hey, when you are gone I will dedicate a fantastic quote to you. Guess what? Come on, ask me, ask me." Doctor's face was close to Pankaj's ear. He was whispering his lines in a slow and deliberate murmur.

"Doctor, get out of my house." Pankaj was getting hysterical.

"The line, on your FB would say; a cat has nine lives, too bad, lion has only four, RIP Pankaj. How do you like it? Isn't that super?" The doctor throated a menacing laughter.

Pankaj cringed with fear.

"Ok, now we are going to play *Kaun Banega Crorepati*. Pankaj, welcome to the show. Pankaj, you are on the hot seat. And sitting here you could make your dreams come true; of leaving this world, this hell, and flying off with your beloved, this pretty fairy named Death. And to facilitate the same, let the side table give you four options.

One - Injection Insulin 300 iu

Two - Injection Scholine iv

Three - Injection Potassium iv

And four - Injection air bubble in artery

Which option would you like to go for?

Pankaj had fear written all over his face as if he could see his death, this time sure shot.

"Pankaj, your time starts now. Oh, I see, you would not be aware of the names and what kind of death they promise to deliver. After all, you are a poet, not a doctor! The first one is insulin-based, this causes a sharp decline in blood glucose levels, making you go into hypoglycemic coma. In no time your organs would start shutting down and phew! The second one, Scholine will be administered through an iv and will attack your respiratory muscles, causing respiratory muscle paralysis, and in thirty seconds you will start sinking. Before I put on the iv, I will give you some anti-depressant, so you will be light-headed, flying and in no time, without any pain, you will join hands with death. No pain, yet gain.

The third will work gently on you, very tenderly, and

before you know what happened, your heartbeat would stop. Peaceful departure. The fourth is a little crude, yet effective. I will put a small air bubble in your artery. It will travel with your blood, go to your heart and brain and burst. Puff, game over. All of them sure shot, no chance of survival. As your doctor and friend I will be here, till you breathe your last. Only after checking your pulse, ensuring there is none, I shall leave."

The doctor looked towards Pankaj. He was now curled on the couch, shivering like a leaf, sweating profusely.

"So Pankaj, which option would you like to go for?"

"Doctor, you bastard, get out of my house. Get out right away. You are bizarre. Who made you a doctor? You are a killer. Get out you bastard, or else I will call the cops."

"Well, if any one would call the cops it would be me. Out of sympathy and assuming you committed suicide out of desperation and lack of choices, I did not inform the cops. I did not want to ruin your career. I am sure you know that attempting suicide is a punishable crime. Should I call the cops and tell them that you have committed this crime not once but four times? Should I?" The doctor pulled out his mobile from his pocket. "Even the number is simple, one, zero zero. Should I dial it?"

"What do you want, tell me? Whatever you want, have it and go away." He was hysterical, sobbing like a child.

"Pankaj, be the man that you claim you are. You called

me over to ensure that death finds you. I have come here for the same. A doctor never leaves till the job is over. I can only go once I have administered the drug and after you have breathed your last. So be a man, choose from the four options and let us get over with it."

Pankaj was pale, devoid of any blood or life. Dr Prakash got up and collected the four packs and meticulously placed them on the table. He walked towards Pankaj.

"You are not being a co-operative patient. And I don't like that. You know I have my ways." The last sentence was menacingly slow and measured.

"Please doc, let me go. Please." He pleaded.

The doctor examined his face closely and went silent for a moment, as if contemplating. Rays of hope kept flashing on and off in Pankaj's eyes. As he was too weak to resist or even push the doctor out of his apartment, he had no choice but to wait for kindness to dawn upon Dr Prakash.

"Pankaj," he murmured. "You are a bad host. I have come to your place for the first time and you have not even offered me a cup of tea. Bad manners." The sarcastic smile spread on his face.

Pankaj was too relieved to get away from his gaze. He jumped off the couch and almost ran towards the kitchen.

"Pankaj." The doctor called him.

"Yes Sir." His response had the tone of surrender.

"By the time you make tea I will decide if you need to

die or live. Sounds fair?" There was no response.

"Oops, you have forgotten to add any sugar." The doctor sipped and placed the cup back on the table.

"Sir, I did."

"Can I get one more spoon of sugar, if you don't mind?"

"Sure Sir." Pankaj ran towards the kitchen again.

"Yeah, tastes better now," the doctor sipped the tea again. "I don't see you enjoying your tea. Won't you accompany your guest?"

Pankaj picked up his cup and took a large sip. The doctor also took another one.

As he did, his eyes scanned Pankaj's face very keenly. Pankaj caught his piercing stare. He felt a shiver crawl up his spine, a steely chill. The doctor's face was getting hard and cold and his eyes were transfixed on Pankaj's forehead.

"Are you feeling a tingling sensation in your body?"

"Sir, please don't scare me." He was literally on his knees.

"Answer me, you jerk." The voice was stern, and the order straight.

"Yes Sir, now that you have said it, I can."

"Can you feel your eyelids getting heavy and your head getting lighter?"

"Yes Sir, I can."

"Good, now you are ready to meet your beloved."

"Sir, what have you done to me? I am feeling drowsy. Sir, please tell me."

"Nothing you asshole, just mixed a sleeping pill while you were in the kitchen getting sugar. In few seconds you will sleep and then I will administer the injection, making you meet your beloved. Sure shot, no chance of failure."

He got up from the stool and took one of the boxes. Pankaj was howling like a baby. The doctor put a finger to his lips.

"Shhh, you filth, I am going to use the best way, just forty seconds and it will be over. You wretched man, you are not worthy of living. If I could have my way, I would have killed you the second time you had come to my clinic. First time could have been a mistake from your side, but not four times. You have to die."

"Sir, please, I don't want to die. I want to live. I don't want to die. Please Sir." He was crying out loud, sobbing like a girl.

"Too late you stinking piece of shit. Your beloved awaits your arrival." The doctor looked cold and ruthless.

"Sir, give me one more chance. I want to live. I promise I will never bullshit you with poetry or anything. I promise, I will never commit suicide. Please Sir, I want to live, I am scared to die. Forgive me Sir."

The doctor held the syringe in his hands and looked coldly towards him. And then, a yellow trickle spread on the already stained floor.

"Sir, please, don't kill me, I don't want to die." He was sobbing uncontrollably. As his legs were unable to bear the weight of his guilt, he collapsed in the pool of urine created by his fear. "Please Sir, I don't want to die, please. Give me one more chance Sir, please Sir."

The doctor moved back, looked at him, took his bag and walked out of the apartment.

It was only few hours later when a groggy Pankaj opened the boxes. He realised that all the four were empty.

ෂ❖න

The Black Widow

There was nothing much to do as his line manager was on leave. The formal induction occupied first half of the day. Since then he had been looking around, hoping that someone would notice him and give some work.

It was Ajit's first day at Amadeus—his new work place. It was also a travel agency, but bigger than his last office. With more than two hundred employees in the branch he had joined, and thirty offices across the country, the company was on a major expansion spree. His hiring was a result of the same. He was hired for inbound sales.

It was three o' clock. He had to do something for the remaining two hours or so. The HR executive had already handed him the laptop, mobile phone, the new SIM card, access card and visiting cards. He was customizing his new laptop with additional free software, sneaking a look into his Facebook account and also messaging his parents and friends, telling them of his new telephone number.

It was a long, boring day and as expected, he was tired. After coming from office, he re-adjusted his modest dwelling, washed the bed sheet, made himself some eggs and toast and made a few calls. It was late and he was ready to wind up the day. Suddenly his phone rang. It surprised him a little as he had already spoken with his parents in Ranchi and his only two friends in Delhi. No one else had this number.

He looked at the screen to identify the caller. *Jaan*, the screen said.

It confused him. When he had got the phone, as a habit he had checked the contact list. It was empty. Then how come the screen was flashing '*Jaan*'?"

"Hello."

There was no response.

"Hello." This time, he increased the level of his volume. The line was still silent.

"Hello. Can you hear me?" He repeated himself.

"Sorry for bothering you at this hour." It was some woman at the other end of the line. Ajit was flabbergasted. He did not know how to respond.

"It's ok. I think you have got the wrong number. Haven't you?" He quizzed, not even sure if the question was correct.

"No I haven't. But I'm really sorry. I should not have

called you." The voice was soft and apologetic and the answer confusing.

"Why are you being sorry for no reason?"

"There is a reason, but not known to you."

Ajit got a little curious.

"I don't mind knowing the reason, if that's ok with you." The inquisitiveness had started gnawing.

"No, I don't think you should. You will laugh at me."

"How do you know? Aren't you being presumptuous?" Curiosity was almost killing him now. He sat up and put his back against the wall. As of now, sleep was the last thing on his mind.

"Anyone would laugh." The voice was sweet and young.

"Ok, promise, I won't." Why was he promising her anything, he wondered.

"I was missing my boyfriend."

"I didn't get you." His perplexity was genuine.

"Yes, I was missing him so I called."

"But this is my number and I'm not your boyfriend."

"Yes, I know, you can never be."

"So why did you call me?"

"I told you that I called him. This was his number till a few weeks back."

"What?"

"Yes."

"But this is a company owned number. The company

has all the numbers of this series, I mean 002 to 098."

"He was working with Amadeus."

"Oh." It was his turn to be startled.

"Yes, I have been calling this number for the past few days. It was switched off. Don't know why, I tried today also, and…"

"So why don't you call him on his new number?" He wanted to help her or maybe wanted to end the futile conversation.

There was silence again.

"I am sure if he has left the job here, by now he would have got a new number."

"No."

"Strange, these days you get a new number in no time. Why wouldn't he get one?" While rattling off his logic, he thought maybe her boy friend was avoiding her. He had been in a couple of relationships himself where he was forced to change his number and then never share the new one.

"He doesn't need a number now."

Ajit laughed. "Ma'am, please don't mind my saying this, but you are wasting your time calling on this number. I am sure he would have got a new number by now. Only he is not sharing it with you."

"Dead people don't share phone numbers." If silence could screech, it precisely did that, then. The phone, which was balanced precariously between his ear and shoulders, fell off.

"Sorry, I didn't get you ma'am."

"He is dead." She whispered coldly.

"What? Sorry, I did not get you. Who?" He was not too sure of her last line.

"Deba is no more. He is dead."

"Who?"

"My boy friend."

A lump formed in his throat and he cursed himself for jumping his guns. "I am sorry Ma'am."

"It's my destiny, not yours. Sorry for bothering you with all this."

"Not at all Ma'am. And I'm really sorry. Also, apologies for whatever I said to you regarding him not sharing his new number."

"You need not apologize."

"I do, I should have been more careful with my words."

"That's ok. And I'm Devyani."

"Hi Ma'am, I am Ajit. Pleasure talking to you."

"My name is Devyani, not Ma'am." She giggled, shedding her remorse in no time.

"Sorry Ma'am, I mean Devyani." Ajit was surprised at the sudden shift of the conversation. Just a moment back, she was playing the unfortunate lover but now….

"You know Ajit, this number is the only thing I have left of him."

Ajit did not know what to say.

"We were seeing each other for almost two years. He wanted to marry me. He joined Amadeus and was so happy. With his new increased salary, he was sure of marrying me."

"Then?"

"Well, we were coming on his bike; it slipped and God knows what hit him, he died on the spot. He was so fond of bikes."

"Oh."

"I was also hurt. They cremated him while I was still in the hospital. I could not even see him." She started crying.

"Ma'am, please. It is ok, Ma'am. Please don't cry." He had no clue what he was supposed to do.

"I miss him so much, I miss Deba so much." She lamented while he preferred being silent.

"Ajit, would you mind if at times I call this number? Calling this number makes me feel good."

"By all means Ma'am. Is there anything else I can do for you?"

"Yes."

"Please let me know." He was more than willing.

"Stop calling me Ma'am." She giggled again.

They both laughed, albeit Ajit's laughter had undercurrents of confusion.

***

The next day Ajit spoke to Sankalpita, the HR girl, about Deba. She confirmed that the number was earlier with Debashish, so was the laptop which now was given to him. She recalled that he was a sweet Bengali guy, in his late twenties. However, his performance was not up to the mark, therefore at work, he was undergoing a bad time. After this part of the homework, Ajit logged on to Facebook and checked out his page. He found him to be quite an average looking guy. However the real reason for his logging on the page was different—he wanted to have a look at Devyani's picture. Too bad, her picture was nowhere.

His line manager was back and so the grind started. He was given his weekly, monthly and quarterly targets. In no time he was also handed over the hot prospects list and was told to get on with it without wasting any time. The day went by. There was no time to think of anything but work. He reached home late and tired and thought of hitting the bed, without any dinner.

His phone rang; it was "*Jaan*" again.

After the last night's conversation, Ajit had thought of checking the phone if it had any entry saved by that name. But then amidst the morning rush and work, it slipped his mind. Now, he was in two minds, to answer or not.

"Hello."

"Hi, hope I'm not disturbing you."

"No, its perfectly fine." He tried sounding courteous

yet a little withdrawn.

"How was your day?"

"Nothing much. Have been assigned my targets today."

"Have you got Deba's seat?" She sounded excited.

"I am not sure. But I have got his laptop and phone."

" Wow. So you have been hired in his place. Right?" Her exuberance was evident.

"I think so." He was finding it hard to maintain his matter of fact façade.

"Then you would have got his target and territory also."

"In all probability." The chink in his armor was inevitable.

"I'm so excited. You have his laptop, phone, workstation, targets and territory. It is like he is back. Though complex, but for sure there is some reason to feel happy about."

He felt a little nervous. A creepy sensation swept over him.

"You know what Ajit, if you have got everything that belonged to him, don't you think you should get his girlfriend too?" He was too stunned to react. She laughed.

The humor missed him as it was replaced by fear.

"Ma'am, don't you think it's late?"

"Oh, so you don't want his girlfriend?" she prompted.

He got embarrassed, as he was not used to such flirtatious conversations.

"It's not that Ma'am."

"I am not forcing you. But surely you are being cruel." She teased mercilessly.

"What did I do?" He could not help but ask.

"Don't have me as your girlfriend but at least don't insult by addressing me as Ma'am. Remember, you had promised not to use the term Ma'am?"

"Yes, I do."

"So then say my name, Ajit."

"How was your day?" He tried changing the topic.

"No, first say my name."

"What is this?"

"Nothing, just a conversation where you are supposed to use my name. Say it Ajit." She pleaded, seductively.

"Devyani." He spelled it out.

"Gosh, after weeks someone has said my name, from the same phone number, with the same intensity. Say it again Ajit."

He was getting psyched.

"I'm waiting, Ajit." The voice was getting heavy.

"Devyani, it is …"

"Saying the name can't be a sin. Can it? You know, Deba used to call me DivyaDeba. He thought it sounded romantic. Do you feel the same?"

"Yes I guess so."

"How does DivyaAjit sound?"

"What?" He shrieked, "This is not right."

"What?"

"The game we are getting into."

"But how can a game be wrong? After all, it's just a game."

"But…" he hesitated.

"Don't you like games?"

"I do."

"Are you afraid of them?" She tormented.

"Me, afraid of games? No, not at all." He tried putting on a brave front.

"But it seems that you are." She challenged.

"I'm not."

"Or is it you don't like playing with me?" She instigated.

"No, it's nothing like that." He was dropping his guard.

"Are you shy of saying my name, Ajit?"

"No, why should I be?"

"Then say it, Ajit."

"Devyani." It took him a lot of effort.

"Oh Ajit, you are killing me."

"Devyani." He repeated.

"Ajit, I'm melting. Are you liking this game?"

"Yes, Devyani. For some reason, I am. Are you?"

"I'm loving it, Ajit."

"Devyani, do you feel nice talking to me?"

"Yes Ajit, I do."

"Do you, Ajit?"

"Yes, Devyani."

"How tall are you, Ajit?"

"5 feet 7 inches"

"Deba was also of the same height."

"Are you fair, Ajit?"

"No, wheatish."

"Same as Deba."

"You like bikes?"

"Yes, I do."

"He also did."

"Devyani."

"Ajit, it seems that I have got my Deba back."

"Devyani."

"Ajit."

"Devyani, something is happening to me."

"What?"

"I am getting warm, all over, my heartbeat is getting erratic, and my pulse is throbbing."

"Ajit."

"Devyani, what are you doing?"

"It is not me, but us. I am feeling the same ache, the dull throb."

"Devyani."

"Ajit, would you mind if I call you Deba?"

***

Days passed and with each passing day, the duration and the content of the calls kept on getting longer and intense. After having late night conversations with Devyani, he found it impossible to concentrate on work. He tried getting away from her, but it seemed as if he was addicted to her and the conversation. The unusual part was that throughout the day, he would not even think of her. But as the sun went down, she started playing on his mind. The compulsion was getting so heady that Ajit yearned to reach home so that he could get on a call with her. No movies, socializing or outings, nothing. One day, when his boss invited him over to his place, he feigned the onset of viral. His performance was slipping.

***

"Sit down."

Ajit took the chair. It was his monthly review and he was scared.

"Ajit, there is nothing much to talk about. The numbers have not started moving."

"Sir, I know. I will try harder."

"You know, when I hired you, I had great expectations. I still know that you can do wonders. You are young, aggressive, talented, then why?"

"Sir, it was my first month. Maybe I need to change my strategy."

"Yes Ajit, you have to." His line manager nodded. "Don't get me wrong but as your manager I'm responsible to bring out the best in you. It is my professional and social obligation to put you on the right track. And I will do whatever it takes to make you deliver."

"Sure Sir, I'm with you."

"No Ajit, you are not with me. You are with someone else."

"I did not get you, Sir." He had a reason to be shocked.

"As a routine exercise, we check the phone records of our employees, especially the ones in sales. Your phone record brings out one number where you talk every evening, for long hours. I know it is none of my concern, but the effect of these late night calls is turning out to be my problem. I won't enquire if she is your girlfriend or not, but with a sleep of three hours, you will never be able to give your best."

***

"DivyaDeba" He whispered.

"Yes, Deba."

"You are the only thing I want."

"Really?"

"Yes, DivyaDeba."

"Oh Deba, I love you, I love you baby."

"DivyaDeba, I love you too."

"Deba, you know you have not even seen me."

" 'Cause you are such a tease. Haven't I asked for your picture? Do you ever send it?"

She laughed, a throaty laughter. "My Deba really wants to see me, baby?"

"Yes baby, I do."

"What would he do if I let him see me?"

"I would capture your visual in my eyes, in my being, and fill every bit of me with you."

"Oh Deba, you are so intense. You know, I ache for you, you and only you."

"DivyaDeba, I ache for you too." Ajit moaned.

"Deba." She moaned.

"Yes."

"Kiss me."

"Where?"

"All over, kiss your DivyaDeba all over."

"Oh baby, let me."

"Deba?" She suddenly had the abrupt, quizzical tone.

"Yes, what happened?"

"Stop."

"See, how you tease me. First you ask me to kiss you and when I'm turned on, you stop me."

"My sweet baby. I was thinking of a plan. A plan for you."

"Really? What plan?" He sounded excited.

"Would you like to meet me?"

"What? Gosh, I'm dying to, don't you know?" He couldn't control his eagerness.

"Really?"

"Yes baby."

"Would you like to meet me tomorrow?"

"Are you sure?"

"I am. Are you?" She hissed.

"Where?" Ajit was unable to bear the suspense any longer.

"What if I invite you over to my place?"

"I would die for you."

"You liar. All men are."

"I'm not, DivyaDeba."

"So you mean you can die for me."

"You bet."

"Ok, will let you know when you need to die. But right now I need you for something else. So be there at my place, tomorrow, 9 pm."

***

Dear Team,

With great grief, I share the news of the sad demise of Ajit Kumar, in a road accident. His bike skidded and he was hit by a speeding truck. His last rites will be performed today evening, 5 pm, at the Lodhi Road crematorium.

Amadeus family prays for the peace of his soul.

Manager, HR

Amadeus

***

Rajat got into his bed. Being his first day at work, mentally it was very exhausting. He wanted to sleep on time so that he was fresh for the new day.

Suddenly his phone rang. He looked at the screen and it said '*Jaan.*'

Strange, he thought. When the phone was handed to him, he did check the phone directory. It was empty.

"Hello."

"Hello."

"I'm sorry for calling you up so late." A female voice was on the other end of the line.

The Lion, The Leopard
And The Hyena

"Yes, I'm with my boss. Yeah, in Navi Mumbai. Will take at least three hours or maybe more. How many times will you call asking me the same? I will call you once I start from here. Have your dinner and go to bed. I have the duplicate keys."

"Sorry, Sir."

"What for?"

"The call took longer than expected."

"Your girlfriend?"

"Yes Sir."

"Hmmm."

"Sir, we have been seeing each other for the past three years. Recently we have moved in together."

"Is she good in bed?"

"Sorry Sir?"

"Don't act dumb."

"I mean she is my girlfriend, also my fiancée."

"And who told you that girl friend or fiancée is not supposed to be good in bed?"

"Sir, don't you think the question is personal?"

"Don't you think the twenty-nine minutes which your girlfriend violated for no rhyme or reason was personal to me too?"

"I am sorry."

"What for?"

"For wasting your time."

"I feel sorry that you are wasting yours."

"What makes you say so, Sir?"

"Your apprehensive face."

"What about my face?"

"Your phone rang and you went pale and limp."

"It is not that Sir."

"I know it is more."

"I am not getting you, Sir."

"You are proving your existence, your loyalty, your dedication to your girl, every moment."

"Is it wrong?"

"Is it right?"

"But she is my fiancée. If she calls me, is worried for me, what is the hassle?"

"Ask yourself."

"What?"

"Ask yourself if she calls out of care, fear or lack of faith."

"I am sure, out of care."

"Then why does she insist that you have your conversation sitting right where you are when she calls you?"

"She doesn't want me to take the trouble of going out for answering her calls."

"No, she wants to hear the ambient sounds so that she can corroborate the story you would give her."

"I didn't get you, Sir."

"Don't bother, some day you will."

"I love her, Sir."

"Then why tell me?"

"I mean I wanted you to know that we are in love."

"Has your mom ever asked you if you love her?"

"Why should she?"

"Then why should your girl ask the same?"

"Well…"

"Do you tell your mom twenty times in a day how much you love her?"

"No one does."

"Then why does every boyfriend tell the same to his girlfriend or husbands tell the same to their wives?"

"Well…"

"Well, because all is not well and surely love is in the well."

"Does telling how much you love someone amount to being stupid?"

"Don't you feel the same every time you force yourself to say it?"

"Sir, can I ask you something?"

"I have never been in love."

"How did you know that I was about to ask you this question?"

"Remember, 'stupid' being the only constant in any relationship equation?"

"How come you have never been in love?"

"Another beer?"

"Sure Sir."

"Excuse me, two Buds please."

"Yes Sir, how come you have never been in love?"

"What is love?"

"Well…"

"You can do better."

"I mean, love is…"

"Come on lover boy, you don't even know what you are into for the past three years?"

"It's hard to explain."

"What is lust?"

"The surge of passion you feel for someone, that desire to get intimate. To share the innermost feeling, the feeling to be one."

"I'm listening."

"Sir, why is it hard to articulate love?"

"You should know better as you are the one who is experiencing love."

"Is lust something wrong?"

"You are a product of love or lust?"

"Well…"

"Holding hands could not have made your mother conceive you."

"I get your point."

"If this entire world is an outcome of lust, how could lust be a sin?"

"I meant, before marriage."

"Is love a sin before marriage?"

"Certainly not! As a matter of fact love before marriage leads to marriage."

"It is lust that leads you to marriage. The channelization of lust is important so that the streets are not infested with bastards."

"Sir, do you hate love?"

"If you knew that there would be no sex after marriage, would you even bother getting married?"

"Yes, I want to care for my girl."

"Then could you explain why the law of the land grants divorce if the husband is not able to satisfy his wife or is an impotent?"

"I don't know."

"Would your girl be happy if you don't fuck her after marriage?"

"Come on, Sir."

"She will seek someone else."

"Hmmm."

"Why are we so conscious of the word lust?"

"Guess that is how we have been groomed?"

"Well, we weren't taught to fuck, or drink either."

"Do you use the words 'I love you' before and after having sex with your girl?"

"I do."

"Have you asked yourself why do you have to say it?"

"I guess…"

"To take the moral stigma out of the act of having sex. If you are having sex and you think you are in love, then it is perfectly fine, but sleeping with someone if you are not in love, is a sin, or so you are made to believe. Bullshit."

"Isn't lust too crude whereas love so beautiful?"

"At least lust can make babies. Better than making castles in the air. Have you seen a lion? Powerful, majestic, aloof, standing atop a cliff, the wind caressing its golden mane."

"Yes Sir, on Discovery Channel."

"When was the last time when you felt like a lion, all powerful, proud and unshakable?"

"Well…"

"Won't you love to feel like one? With no worries on your mind, no one to answer to, no explanation, no stories, just you and you, in your true self, fuck bothered about the world."

"Is it possible?

"Would you like to rule the world rather than be ruled? Walking amidst this world, fearlessly, holding your head high, knowing that the jungle out there is afraid of your power, grit and strength of character."

"How can I?"

"Another beer?"

"Let me order."

"Sir, how can I be a lion?"

"Have some balls, to start with."

"Well, I do have."

"Do you? In that case, start using them."

"How is one supposed to use his...err...balls?"

"By letting the world know that you have a pair of them."

"And how would the world know?"

"When you feel in-power, in-control, when you have a point of view, when you display strength in your words and actions, when you stand up for yourself, your friends, your team, your work, when right is right and wrong is wrong... irrespective of person, place or time, when people look up to you because you don't look down upon them, when grace is not going to the gym and flexing your triceps but that inner strength which empowers you to be fair and honest."

"That's a tall order."

"Small steps will help you achieve them."

"Any opening lines?"

"I won't lie to myself, or to others."

"But then the world would crumble and fall."

"As if the lion cares. He is standing there, atop the cliff, aloof, watching the world pass by."

"Hmmm."

"Won't it make me cold?"

"A sane, cold man is preferred any day over a warm, bumbling idiot."

"Is this lion all about sanity?"

"Strength of character is the key word. Sanity, justice, fairness are manifestations."

"What do I gain being a lion?"

"Your peace of mind, your piece of land, your piece of wisdom, pride, confidence and of course a group of leopards to tame."

"And what do I stand to lose?"

"Hyenas."

"Hyenas?"

"Yes."

"I understand that if I will be a lion, the leader as it would mean in today's context, I will be a fearless leader who will have a dedicated group of followers. But I am not able to get the context of hyenas. Who could be them?"

"Another beer?"

"Aren't we going too fast?"

"Till the time you are not a lion, standing on a cliff, if you slow down you will get hunted."

"In that case I will go for another one."

"Repeat the order, please."

"Are you avoiding my question, Sir?"

"I don't want to hurt a young leopard."

"But if you don't, he will never graduate to being a lion."

"Well said."

"The answer please."

"Some other day, maybe tomorrow."

"If tomorrow comes."

"Truth is brutal."

"Sweet lies are fatal."

"But it is comforting."

"After this conversation with you, I have started hating comfort."

"It could hurt you."

"I don't care."

"You could be shattered."

"I want to be the lion."

"Right now your girlfriend is in bed with someone else."

"What? How dare you? I mean, Sir, what are you saying?" The eyes of the young man lit up with indignation. He choked on his beer to find the right words to address the statement hurled at him.

"It is ok if you feel like abusing me. Truth makes you get in a self-denial mode."

"How can you say this?"

"When you asked her where she was, she said she was in the balcony. And that very moment there was that ping sound of microwave. Surely, with all the traffic in the area, irrespective of the size of the house, that sound should not have been audible."

"Were you eavesdropping?"

"So she lied to you for no reason. That makes her a habitual liar."

"Sir, you are just putting together un-correlated facts to make up a story."

"Forget it. Let us have the beer."

"Am I supposed to take this slandering?"

"Forget it, I apologize. Another beer?"

"But you have no right to defame her. I mean you don't even know her."

"Can we get over this?" His tone was a strange mix of sarcasm, authority and disgust.

"You have hurt me, Sir."

"I will make up for it."

"Sorry Sir, I thought you were trying to guide me. But now it seems that all you wanted was to distance me from her. Maybe you have some hidden agenda."

"Stop being melodramatic."

"You have no right to run her down."

"Just because I'm being polite don't assume truth to flip sides."

"What is your truth? To misguide people, to use them, to make them your followers so that you can rule? You just want to be the lion."

"Guess you are too drunk."

"I'm glad that I am. At least I can speak my mind. You are a manipulator, a master fixer of young minds and nothing else. Now I can see why team members say that you use people to achieve your selfish goals."

"Is there anything else?"

"Yes, I assumed you to be the lion, me the leopard, but the truth is that you are the hyena."

"I think we should call it a day. Just a word of advice; when you get back to your love nest, kiss your girl and see if her earlobes and wrists are dabbed with very sweet, feminine perfume. Then kiss her neck, inhaling deep and see if you get a faint whiff of men's perfume, aftershave or cologne. I am sure you know what I mean."

***

A leopard can never be a lion. No wonder, by the time he reached back home, of course after telling his girl that he had started, he was too drunk to remember anything the real lion had told him.

"Oh baby, you smell so different tonight."

"It is your love that makes me so fragrant, honey." The hyena giggled.

A Rose For Her

Her name was Sati. Although she was not sure of her age but her mother had told her that she would be around ten to twelve years old. Her family lived in a makeshift shack at the pavement itself. She was a poor girl and sold flowers outside a public school, which was located on a busy intersection. The traffic kept her on her toes all day as she would run to offer flowers to every passing car, scooter and rickshaw; even passers-by. Most were too busy to even look at her. But owing to her sweet smile and innocent face, some kind-hearted people did not mind picking up a bunch or maybe a flower or two. Festival times meant good business for her; especially New Year's and Valentine's Day.

His name was Raj and he studied in standard fifth in

the same public school in front of which Sati sold flowers. He was a quiet child who used to walk to school with a school bag slung low on his back, lost in his own world. Unlike other kids, he rarely ran or jumped or expressed his exuberance.

Everyday he would buy a red rose from Sati.

The routine was fixed.

"As always, one bright red rose please." He would say.

"Here you go." Sati would hand him one.

This went on for months.

One day, out of curiosity Sati finally asked him, "Why do you buy a red rose everyday?"

"I buy them for my mother. Roses are her favorite. I keep them on her bedside table. She loves it."

Sati smiled and said, "Your mother is very lucky."

From that day onwards, she would pick the best rose from the lot and keep it aside for Raj. One day Raj gave her a chocolate and said, "It's my birthday and I want to thank you for all the lovely roses which have made my mother very happy."

Sati accepted the token of friendship and felt very good. On reaching home, she flaunted the chocolate to her family before giving each of her brothers a piece.

This went on; seasons changed. Raj was promoted to sixth standard. But whenever he would spot Sati with red roses, he would buy one for his mother.

Suddenly Raj stopped coming to the school. Sati would wait for him with a long stemmed red rose everyday till the school bell rang and the road became vacant. After waiting for a few days, Sati began to worry about him. So she asked Rahul, Raj's best friend. Rahul told her that Raj was unwell and bedridden. Sati decided to pay him a visit.

As she started for his home, she thought since Raj was sick, his mother must have been missing the roses, which he bought for her everyday. She remembered Raj telling her how much his mother loved the flower. Armed with a rose in her hand, she pressed the doorbell of Raj's house.

'Ding dong. Ding dong.'

A servant came out and glared at her and yelled, "Go away, no beggars allowed."

Taken aback, Sati protested, "No, no, I am not a beggar or a thief. I am the flower-seller from the school street. Raj buys flowers from me everyday."

His expression changed. "Oh, Raj is not well. Why are you here?"

"Raj buys a red rose from me everyday for his mother. Since he has not been able to for the last few days, I thought his mother would be sad, so I got a red rose for her." Sati explained innocently.

The servant froze her with an ugly stare and after a moment of quiet inspection, shook his head and said, "What are you saying? His mother died five years ago."

With this, he slammed the door in her face.

With his last words echoing in her ears, Sati stood there, rooted to the ground, staring at the red rose in her hand.

A Highway Called Life

Is life cruel or is it just a reflection of what we want to see? But then who am I to decide it for you? We all have a right to form our own set of opinions and prejudices. So let me be the medium and narrate the incidences of my unusual life. Should I start sequentially or... I think I would rather go with the flow.

Bijoy Sengupta and Lopa Sengupta, with great love and affection named me Piyasi. Yes, you got it right, they are my parents. *Baba*, my father, worked with a law firm as an accountant. He was a tall, dark man with typical Bengali looks—round face, small eyes, soft looks and a small pot belly. Even my mother, who was a homemaker, also carried the trademark Bengali looks—dark, deep eyes, a pretty face and shiny black tresses. For some reason, every day after oiling her flowing and thick hair, she put a red flower in her tight braid. A typical middle-class family, we worshiped Goddess Durga—the deity of power and the destroyer of evil. When I looked at her face, I thought she resembled my mother a lot. Both had the same beautiful eyes, spiritual and endearing faces and both put a big red *bindi* on their foreheads. The similarity did not end there. Even their *sarees* were the same; single color with big border.

It was the night of 13th June that I opened my eyes. Being my parents' first child, they were ecstatic. As we stayed with our grandparents, at their place, even they were overwhelmed. Amidst my own cries, their laughter, compliments and congratulatory notes, the initial days went by.

Life seemed to be rosy.

My grandmother doted on me. From my daily oil massage to bath, telling me stories to knitting small sweaters, she was all over me. She planned to celebrate my birthday with great pomp and show. She went on and on as to how she would plan, who all she would invite, how she would decorate the place, what she would make me wear and her wish list never seemed to end. A few weeks before my birthday, she fell ill. Out of choice, with a heavy heart, she had to postpone the celebration. But there was always the next one.

The day I completed two years, 13th June, was the day for her. All my cousins, maternal grandparents, relatives, neighbors were invited over. It was supposed to be the biggest event in our house after my father's marriage. A lot of dancing, singing and general celebration was happening. I was dressed in a pink frock, a small cap and was wearing a small silver chain. Everybody clapped as I cut my birthday cake. My cousins and the children of neighbours were so excited. They were busy singing, playing and bursting the balloons. In sheer excitement, one of them came to me and burst a big balloon near my ear. I did not react. My grand mother and mother rushed towards the boy who had pulled up the prank. When they came back to me, I could see their faces with a quizzical expression. For some unknown reason, they started clapping near my ear, singing, shouting and finally howling. I could not hear anything. The world was as calm as it was the first day.

The party was called off. Everyone left looking at me, with pity. I was unable to comprehend the reason. I could see my parents and my grandparents clearly tense. My father took me to a building, which was painted white. A woman wearing a white coat came and inspected my ears using weird looking instruments. Ouch, it hurt! She consoled my father and we all left. Our house was silent after that. The activity, the celebration, the exuberance was all gone. My grandmother never came near me and when she did, I could clearly see the scorn on her face.

A week later reports came from the white building. It

said I was deaf and would not be able to hear for life. All hell broke loose. My mother wept inconsolably and started throwing things around. Lying there, in a corner, I watched the changed scenario. My grandmother cursed my mother for bearing a deaf child, my mother cursed number thirteen, which was my birthday, my father cursed the stars and grandfather his past karma. Everyone cursed everyone. I felt scared and so lonely.

Days passed and with each passing day the changes became more and more visible. From being the centre of everyone's joy, now I was an unwanted object in the house. No one wanted to touch me, hold me or play with me. Every one hated me for no fault of mine. It was killing me from inside. I could not hear them but the words were written all over their faces.

One day my mother; my living Goddess, took me to an orphanage and left me there. I quietly sat there on a bench, not even asking for food, though I was famished. Tears would not flow, as there weren't any left. I can still remember the hunger pangs I felt that day. Though I don't know for sure but I assume that when father would have returned from his office he would have asked about me. Not finding me there, he would have forced my mother to tell him about my whereabouts. Holding his finger, walking down the long corridor, that evening I walked out of the orphanage. That walk from the bench to the gate was the longest walk of my life.

Weeks passed away. *Baba* was the only support I had. He took me to a lot of schools in Kolkata. Each and every school denied me admission. With every passing day, I could see the helplessness grow in the eyes of my *Baba*. I loved him a lot. I wanted to do something for him. But then, I was of no use. I was no good. I cherished spending time with him. My only desire was to be with him, near him, around him.

Five years had gone by. After my second birthday, there was no more celebration. But *Baba* remembered that day without fail. He would take me out to Victoria Palace, make me sit on his shoulder, show me the traffic, the cabs, the cops on horseback and the hustle-bustle. He was my world and I loved him.

Agreed, life is not fair but then like everything even that changes. *Baba* found a new job in Bangalore. We all moved to the new city. Bangalore proved to be my turning point. I was able to find a school that took me in with open arms. I started regaining my self-esteem and confidence. My first teacher, Ms Leena Kalapala was my mentor, my *Guru*. I used to address her as *Gurumaa*.She was the one who introduced me to a new world of words, expressions and feelings. She empowered me with a supreme method of communication—how to talk.

I wasn't a good student. However, *Gurumaa* told me that I was a good one. But I knew she was being kind to me. I could barely pass. By this time I had lip-read and written words too. I had four classes a day. The ones, which I really enjoyed, were my art and dance classes. I was passionate about them. *Baba* used to pick me up from the school. After my school, I used to spend time with my favorite person; my *Baba*.

Baba was a good photographer. He taught me how to use his Kodak camera. I was quite amazed at the tricks it had in terms of exposure, aperture and how the same picture could look different by adjusting the settings. I started clicking more and more pictures. People, places, weather, nature, animals, everything was an object for me and I clicked everything.

My grandfather fell sick. We had to move back to Kolkata. I joined the normal day-boarding school in eighth standard. Being naughty and playful, I made lot of good friends. I tried hard comprehending what my new teachers taught me, but my mind was somewhere else. I failed my weekly tests but my photography bloomed. Even my teachers started taking notice of my work. I was appointed as the school photographer for the monthly newsletter.

Life was moving and I was promoted to tenth standard. Life was my friend, a decent friend. And this decent friend never told me what surprise it had for me. There was a photography competition. My picture was selected and sent abroad for external evaluation. Well, the rest as they say is history.

Luckily mine got selected and I was offered a scholarship at St. Mary's—a prestigious photography school in London. That evening, *Baba* hugged me and wept for long. I wept too, holding him. With tear-stained eyes, I could see my mother standing near the door, weeping. She could finally see that physical disability was not a curse.

Is life unfair? Well, as said earlier, the take ought to be yours. To me it is about self-confidence and willingness to follow your heart. In my case, life gave me a shortcoming but then it also blessed me with my *Baba* and *Gurumaa*.

Today, I am a budding photographer working under a top notch, international shutterbug. So never lose heart and hope. Remember, if somewhere there is a roadblock, there ought to be a highway too.

The Chosen One

"You are leading a blessed life, dude."

"I swear, imagine making money doing something that we all dream of day and night."

The whole group burst into laughter, but for Deepak.

"Come on Deepak, don't blush. We envy you."

"Guys, not only him, but I envy his father too. The rocking father-son duo."

Another round of hysterical laughter filled the KFC outlet.

Driving home, Deepak was trying to overcome a gamut of emotions—rage, self-pity and helplessness. Together, they were wreaking havoc on his whole being. Was it his fault if he was born to a father who had the largest lingerie store in the city?

As he stopped at the red light, he looked around. The street was uninhabited. After all, for a city like Hissar, life past 10 pm was largely restricted around television sets or the bedrooms. He hated himself so much for being a part of this small town, his shop and his whole existence.

Since the day he could remember, his house would be stacked with boxes of bras, panties, sleepwear and other lacey stuff. Nonchalantly, his father would open the boxes, pull out random pieces and rub them between his fingers, feeling the fabric, holding it close to his eyes, inspecting the stitch quality and at times pulling at the elastic band to see if the material used was as promised by the vendor. There were times when he was forced to think of his father as a pervert. After all, how could a man spend his entire day and life around lingerie?

This was before he joined him, albeit with disgust and contempt. He vividly remembered his first day at the shop when a lady asked for thirty-six 'C' cup. He was petrified handing over the box with the size asked for. And then his father entered the scene.

"*Behanji*, how are you? Haven't seen you in here for long? Hope you are not annoyed with me? Let me show you something very exclusive. I have just got this consignment from China. A piece of art. Best quality cotton, with high grade elastic and completely seamless. Deepak, show *behanji* the Little Daisy box. *Behanji*, I am sure you would love it."

For days, weeks and months, his life revolved around his shop—Saundarya, showcasing various kinds and sizes of bras and panties. Now he was also quite a connoisseur on the subject. He could tell how to measure the cup size correctly, which fabric would suit a particular weather and outfit, the difference between wired, strapless and sports bra. Women of the city loved having a young guy sell them what was their well-guarded secret. Some of his clients even started hitting onto him. But he only had one feeling for the whole goddamn show; that of condescension.

The whole business of selling undergarments had affected his mind too. There were times when he would get dreams of women asking him to measure their cup size and then parading in front of him, wearing crotchless panties and thongs. Surprisingly, he would get up not with an erection but with a desire to throw up, which he did at times. He would often squirm in a daze, hoping to find an escape. For a guy his age, eighteen, he was undergoing too much of an emotional trauma. Whenever he would see a woman, he would start imagining the kind of bra, the size of bra she would be wearing, along with the kind of panty.

While his friends talked about college life, girls, parties, outings, he had little to contribute to the conversation. Without their knowing, he had become a laughing stock. He remembered the day when he had gone out with his school time friends and one of them introduced him to his girlfriend.

"Deepak, what do you do?" Suman asked.

"He is our idol. He measures the cup sizes of women. He can even tell what is yours." His friend interjected.

He could do nothing but turn red, with embarrassment and shame.

***

"*Maa*, I want to take up a job." His declaration was out of the blue.

"What happened?" The kind mother enquired, ruffling his hair and placing another *aloo paratha* on his plate.

"Nothing, but I want to do something new."

"*Beta*, you know your father. He will never agree, and what problem do you have here? At your age you have a fully established business on your hands?"

"*Maa*, I don't want to sell those things anymore. I don't like it." He sullenly pushed the *paratha* on his plate.

She went silent for a while. "Your father started selling clothes when he was only twelve. Later he saved for a bicycle and loaded all the clothes in a battered suitcase, which had to be tied to the rear carrier. He pedaled for hours in the sun, house-to-house, selling suit-length, *dupattas* to ladies in the city. He worked very hard and today he has his own air conditioned shop and is doing so well."

"*Maa*, I have heard this story umpteen number of times. You call this doing well? I mean how could anyone sell such stuff all their life?" Deepak was embarrassed to mention the words bra and panty in front of his mother.

"What do you want to do?" She just wanted the conversation to end.

"I want to join a call center." His announcement was well-rehearsed. "They pay well and we have a good call center in our city too."

"Is that what you want to do?" His mother was irritated.

"Yes." He seemed convinced.

"*Beta*, we all have been assigned a role. It is all pre-decided what we will do in our lives. If we can seek satisfaction in playing that role, only then we can find peace and happiness." Her two statements had the essence of life but for some reason they infuriated her son.

"*Maa*, I don't know what you are saying. But surely my role in life can't be selling lingerie. And even if it is, I will change it." He banged the plate with the half eaten *paratha* and walked out of the dining room.

***

"So you never went to college?"

"No Sir."

"And may I know the reason?" The interviewer leaned towards him. Dressed in a crisp white shirt and purple tie, to Deepak, he looked very cool. Sitting in the big conference room of Advent; the multi-national call center with more than twenty thousand employees, Deepak ached to be a part of the set-up at any cost. On his way to the conference room, he had seen smart guys and pretty girls, sitting on bean-bags, holding colorful coffee mugs and having a nice time.

"Sir, my father wanted me to help him in his business."

"That's nice. What business do you have?"

"Sir, we are into garments." His eyes quickly diverted to the painting behind the interviewer. A little lie never killed anyone.

"Interesting. Some day I will come over to your shop. Hope you will give me some discount."

They both laughed.

***

"Good morning, Sir. Welcome to La Care, the largest lingerie store in Europe. This is Shaun David. How may I help you?"

"Well, I was on your site and have certain queries."

"Sure Sir. I would request if you could be a little more specific."

"I would like to buy from your site."

"That is nice to know Sir. What would you like to order?"

"Well, a pair of bra and panty."

"Sir, if I may know the preference I shall be in a position to help you better."

"I want to buy your product number LCBR 098 and LCPN 4465 along with LCBR 4432 and LCPN 8861."

"Very well Sir, could you mention the required sizes?"

"34B for LCBR098, medium for LCPN 4465, 36C for LCBR 4432 and large for LCPN 8861."

"Very well Sir. I hope you have seen the colors of the products and you understand that you are ordering for different sizes."

"Why don't you place the order?" The caller was getting on the offensive.

"Sir, it is my duty to let you know. I assumed that being a male, you would be having a little handicap."

"Could you place the order please?"

"Sure Sir. That would be five thousand and fifty five only. What payment option would you like to choose?"

"COD."

"That would be nice Sir. Can I have your name and the delivery address please?"

" Rajesh Jain, 1/43, Rohtas Nagar, Near Railway Station, Hissar, Haryana, India."

***

"What happened to your new job?"

"Nothing papa."

"Ok listen, just in case I am not here, please receive a packet which will come from La Care. Pay them five thousand and fifty five. I have ordered four products as sample. Once you receive it, courier them to our Bahjanpura vendor in Delhi and ask him how soon he can send us something similar at one tenth of the cost."

Though it took him a while but Deepak had learnt the lesson of being the chosen one, taught by his mother. If being Shaun David too lead him to the world of lingerie, where he was supposed to discuss bra and panty over the call with his father, then he might do the same within the confines of his own shop.

Home Sweet Home

"Be careful. It has crockery in it." He shrieked. "I don't know what all you will break."

The man sounded distressed. In his late fifties, dressed in a white pajama and a vest, for the past two days he had been facing a harrowing time. After all, shifting a complete household of thirty years was no mean feat. The ordeal was further complicated because he was forced to do it all by himself.

Much against his own wishes, he had hired a movers and packers agency to reduce his hassle. But it seemed that they were too focused on completing the task rather than completing it well. They were too callous and mechanical to note that the refrigerator could get an extra scratch, or the glass plates could break. Though they had told him that they were in control and knew exactly what they were doing, but somehow he was not convinced with their robotic actions.

Sitting on a stool, he looked around at the workers, who wrapped, packed, and moved his dream house like men who were possessed. He hated their apathetic movements. How he wished they could know what it took to build the house, spending hours, even days selecting everything, from the writing table to the bed, cutlery to the fans. For them it was just another house, but for him it was his home, his only home.

He got up from the stool and walked towards the balcony. The flowerpots had been moved away, few ants looked confused in the remnant grime, perhaps because they were used to the cold dark crevice under the moist pots. Apart from a pile of newspapers, there was nothing there. But he wanted to be sure. So he went inside the dining hall and pulled the stool out. The stool was his only friend from this household, which had not been packed. He still remembered that he had bought it from one of the roadside shops on his way back from his office. It had been almost fifteen years and it had stood the test of time. He put the stool in the balcony and stood on it, looking in the small recess, which the AC opening had to its side. That was the place, where he used to hide his cigarettes. Malti hated the pack of his brand, Gold Flake. On several occasions, the packet had been the source of many altercations; some of them serious too. He would quit smoking but then get back to it. Even after embarking on an exhaustive research and reasoning exercise, he could never figure out why it was so hard for him to quit. What was smoking? Simply put, inhaling the smoke. How could inhaling smoke be pleasurable? He knew that it was a waste but then he could not figure out why he was wasting money, health and peace of mind.

Today, he just hoped to find some old packet hidden in there. A cigarette would be so good amidst all the chaos. At that precise moment he ached to stand there, in his balcony, and to have a smoke, maybe for the last time.

As he stood on his toes, peeping into the recess, he could see a few straws. He had no clue how could straws get in there. He was tempted to insert his hand but then the thought of a snake or a lizard taking a nip off his finger stopped him. He descended from the stool and entered the almost empty living room.

His eyes looked around for the small wooden ladder, which the movers and packers were using to remove the ceiling fans. There it was, lying in a corner. He hurried towards it. Was it supposed to be that heavy or was he getting old, he thought as he hoisted the ladder on his shoulders. Balancing it on his aching shoulders, he walked out in the balcony and placed it urgently against the wall. He was panting. He was getting old and he knew it. He adjusted the ladder against the wall and climbed up. The ladder creaked.

He was scared. At his age, hip fracture was the last thing that he wanted. He climbed up, securing the ladder with his hands and peeped in, expecting the worst. As his eyes adjusted to the relative darkness of the recess, he could see a small nest in there. God, he made all the effort to see a nest? He cursed himself, while hoisting himself higher, ascending one more rung of the ladder.

The nest had two beautiful eggs. White and smooth. It was the first time he was seeing eggs in a nest. For a moment, the white eggs against the brown twigs and hay mesmerized him. He looked around to see if the mother was anywhere in sight. But he had no clue which bird to look for. Looking at the size of the eggs, he assumed that they belonged to pigeons. Not that he was some authority on birds, but then he was free to guess.

"Sir, what else needs to be packed?" The worker shouted.

"Start packing the bedroom also." He replied while admiring the sight.

***

"But as per the terms and conditions, I have paid seventy percent of the money."

"You have, I am not debating it, but others haven't."

"But that does not mean that you won't hand over my apartment on time."

"Sir, till the time it gets completed, gets a certificate of completion, a worthiness certificate, the possession can't be made."

"What about your penalty clause? The contract did say that if the possession was not made within sixty months, you would pay a penalty."

"You are right, but if buyers are not paying the money, how are we supposed to complete the project?"

"I have been coming here for seven years now. At least suggest some way out."

"See, buyers like you have already filed a case. I would suggest that you wait for the court's verdict."

***

"What happened?" Malti was concerned, intently watching his depressed face.

"Can I have some water?"

"You don't worry. Leave it. We will think that we don't yet deserve the new house."

"Do you think it is as easy as that?" He got up from the cane chair. "I have put in all of my hard earned money. It has been ten years that we have been waiting for our own home."

"But we can't have the desire of our own home at the cost of your health." She sounded concerned.

"I will not sit patiently." He fumed.

"What will you do?"

"I will go and meet the media. I know they will have

it fixed."

"As if they are waiting only to listen to your complaint." She handed him a glass of water.

"Everyone is scared of the media, even the prime minister is. I have talked to someone who knows someone at *Dainik Jagran*, I will go there tomorrow."

"See, we have been living in this house for almost thirty years now. Fortunately, we have a landlord who is so nice. It is like our own place." Malti tried to explain to him in the calmest possible tone.

"But this is not our place." He got up and walked out.

***

"Why do you have to get swayed by false promises and claims?" The journalist was annoyed.

"But…"

"I mean, do you think any builder can give you a three room apartment for sixteen lacs?"

"The company was registered. The legal bodies should have taken a note of the same."

"Sir, please don't mind, but in a country as big as India, if the law starts taking a note of every single thing, we would be going nowhere. Why can't we, as alert citizens, also take care of our interest?"

"I am surprised that you are also on their side." He was crestfallen.

"I am on the side of law. I have seen the documents. Leave this file with me. I will call the builder and have a word with our lawyer too."

***

"Any luck?"

"Yes, he said that he would speak to the builder and get his lawyer's opinion."

"Some water for you?" Malti walked towards the kitchen.

"Malti, at times I feel so lost. What wrong have I done? I have paid my taxes, never got on the wrong side of the law, booked an apartment, which was approved by the authorities. As per the payment plan, I gave them the money and yet there is no one who can listen to my complaint. Why? Am I too weak or is it the system?"

"Don't worry, everything will be all right." She smiled. "Today I have made your favorite *aloo-gobhi* and *roti*."

***

"My wife is suffering from cancer. I need the money."

"You have my sympathies, but how can I give you any money?"

"I don't want the apartment. Please return my money."

"I am sure you understand that I can't. But if you want I can help you in finding a buyer." The builder offered his conditional compassion.

"Do you think there would be any buyer for a project which has been on hold for ten years?"

"I can only try."

"I don't know why I trusted you guys with my hard earned money."

"I never came to you seeking your money. This is just another occupational hazard. It happens. If you had got the apartment, at this price, it would have been a steal and you would have felt like a king. Too bad, the project got stalled."

***

Out of nowhere a pigeon flew in. Upon seeing him, perched on the ladder, near the recess, it stopped midair and flapped hard to break its momentum and speed. The flutter of wings disrupted his chain of thoughts. He looked at the two white eggs safely encased in the small nest. His eyes shifted to the pigeon that was encircling near him. His jawbones hardened. He looked back at the eggs again and hollered. "Where are you guys, come over here. Get all the stuff back. I am not shifting yet."

***

"Malti, I know you will think that I have lost it. But after going through the trauma of trying to have a house of our own, there was no way I would have let the pigeons face the same. Do you still think I'm stupid? I can always shift once they grow up and leave for their abode. In any case, I have waited twelve years for the house. Now that it is ready, what is the hurry? I can shift anytime. After all it is my house, I mean, our house. "

From the garlanded picture frame, Malti smiled, or so he thought.

The Other Side

"Tuktuk" she hollered, "get up or else you will be late for school."

Maya got back to the screen of her laptop, her eyes scanning every single contact on her Facebook friend list. As her eyes probed them, mentally she made a note of the criteria, which she had in mind. Some twelve hundred plus friends and not even one who could be of any use to her? She mumbled to herself, "Goddam! Why is it called a friend list, all bloody cold acquaintances."

"Have you left the bed?" She logged out of Facebook, shut down her laptop and walked towards Tuktuk's room.

The bed was empty and she could hear water running in the adjoining washroom. She heaved a sigh of relief. Getting Tuktuk, her six year old daughter ready for her school was a daily ordeal. But then she consoled herself that every mom had to face the same.

She tied her hair in a tight bun and hurriedly walked towards the kitchen. There was a lot on her mind. Preparing vermicelli for Tuktuk's breakfast, packing her tiffin; with one boiled egg, a piece of bread cut diagonally turned into a sandwich, with a mixture of butter and jam in between and then making oats for herself. Diligently, she set about starting her morning chores. Suddenly she walked out of the kitchen, towards her bedroom. She looked around and was incensed.

"Have you taken my phone again? How many times have I told you not to use it for Angry Birds." She stomped towards Tuktuk's room. As she entered the room, her eyes saw the Blackberry lying on the bed. Hastily, she picked it up and plodded towards the kitchen.

The water in the pan with a solitary egg was boiling but she was too engrossed in composing a message. As soon as the message was sent, she shifted her attention back to the pan. The knife deftly sliced the bread. As an act of kindness, after cutting it in two, she applied some butter and jam on the piece of bread.

The phone beeped. She grabbed it with a sense of urgency. The content of the message exasperated her. She chewed the side of her lips and composed another one. As an afterthought she added the names of two more recipients and pressed the send button. A pair of scissors sliced the oat packet and she poured the entire content in a small pan. Before adding water, she liked to roast the oats first. Anticipating her phone to beep, she looked at it longingly. Too bad, technology did not respond to her whims.

She opened the refrigerator and pulled out a small saucer with her daily dose of turmeric, rose water and a little cream. The fingers knew the contours of her face well. In long, gentle strokes they applied the potion covering her cheeks, forehead and neck. She looked at the phone again. Her restlessness was growing. The pan with roasted oats was simmering. She stirred the pan using a ladle.

"Tuktuk, hurry up, you will miss your bus."

Maya picked her phone again, checking for any response. Frustrated, she composed another one, this time adding five recipients. Standing there in the kitchen, she held the phone, staring at the screen, waiting for it to respond. Nothing happened. She bit the side of her lower lips again. Her ears were turning warm. She could feel the surge in her grow. Holding Tuktuk's water bottle under the RO tap, she stared at the solitary marigold in the tub. She tried to loosen her muscles for a few seconds; and her finger turned moist and warm. "Heck, no." Water was overflowing from the bottle into her hands and on the kitchen slab. "Heck again! Damn you all," she sweared.

Wiping the spilt water, she dialed a number but then

disconnected the call. Maybe it was too early for a call. Her thumb scrolled on the track ball of her Blackberry, going through the contact list. She stopped at one and composed a message again. The send button was pressed again.

Twenty minutes to six, the cuckoo clock on the kitchen wall cautioned her. Maya walked towards the bedroom and pulled out a pink towel from her wardrobe and stepped towards the washroom. She walked in, bolted the door and then again flung it open, stepped out, wrapped in her towel. She looked at her phone, which was lying on the bed and took it with her to the washroom.

***

"The kid had a little lamb,
going up the hill,
moves fast and slow,
but never comes to a still."

"Very good. Now at school, you have to recite the same poem confidently." Maya instructed Tuktuk.

Beep Beep.

The phone came to life. Hurriedly and with her heart pounding, she checked the screen.

"Bastard." Without wasting any time, she composed another message.

"Mommy, where are we going this Sunday?" Tuktuk looked up, scanning her mom's face for an affirmative answer.

"If you score an A in recitation, maybe I will take you to McDee and treat you to your favorite McMeal."

Beep Beep

Maya checked her phone again. She could feel her cheeks and ears turn red as she replied to the message, biting her lower lips.

***

Sitting in her cubicle, she could feel the restlessness grow. With every passing minute, her body was feeling the stress. She opened her Facebook page again, playing with a solitary lock of hair on her temple. As she scanned her friend list once again, her eyes kept on scurrying between the laptop and the phone screen. She checked the status on her office chat engine, making sure it was 'green'; she typed a name to check status – offline. Damn!

A small bead of sweat trickled down her neck. She opened the bottle and took a large sip. Maybe, it would help her dehydrated throat. Her mind was not able to focus on any task. For the last two days, work was piling up on her desk. There were at least fifty e-mails, which needed her attention. She opened her mailbox and tried to focus. But then failed. She composed a new e-mail, wrote two lines, and then with a firm shake of her head, sent it to the recycle bin.

She got up and scanned the floor. With some two hundred odd people; for sure there would be a way out.

Think positive, she told herself and decided to take a walk. Maybe, she would have lady luck by her side.

The weight of her forty-year-old frame balanced precariously on the stilettos was pulling her down. Though the carpeted floor was absorbing the tell-tale signs of her anxious steps, but her mind was reverberating with the same. With every step, the echo of her own self was multiplying inside her. Every step had an ounce of hope and a pound of failure.

Her eyes were too busy darting across the cubicles, searching for that one positive indication, that sign. Which dark hole was consuming her messages? Or was she being consumed?

***

Well, maybe she should try during the lunch hours, her mind told her.

Yeah, after all that was the only time when people were a little less formal and in their spirits. Her incessant chew on her lips was growing.

Thursday, Friday, Saturday, Sunday and today was Monday. God, four days! Or was it five or six? She tried doing the calculation again.

The sweat was trickling down with more vigor. She opened her bag and pulled out a small bottle. As she unscrewed the cap, she reminded herself of calling the doctor. Two pills pushed down her system and she hoped some magic would work.

She dialed the contact saved as 'Doc.'

"Hi, this is Sudha. I am not in town and will be back only on Wednesday. Please leave your name and phone number and I will get back as soon as I can. Good day."

Damn, she cursed herself and the doctor.

Her lips had started to quiver. She stretched her back and could feel a nervous tingling crawl up her backbone. What would follow was well known to her. She had to fight it. She would not lose it today, she told herself. Ignoring the curious looks of the cleaning staff, she looked at herself very intently in the washroom mirror. As she held on to the edge of the basin, she used all her strength to contract every possible muscle in her body, till everything was in a tight knot at the base of her stomach. Then gradually released her breath, and along with it the pent up energy and apprehensions. She kept staring at herself wondering if this really made her feel any better!

***

"Hi, where have you been?" She tried being saccharine sweet.

"Don't even ask me. My in-laws are here and life is totally screwed up. With year closing and a demanding set of in-laws, can't even check my personal mail."

"So where is Rohit?"

"Oh, him? He has been travelling. He always scoots from the *saas-bahu* drama! " Maya knew that this was a case where she wouldn't find her way as well. She excused herself on pretext of fetching a print out.

Her feet were getting cold and her head was getting lighter. A weird daze was settling in when she was nodding to people, smiling at acknowledgements without actually registering her environment. She composed another message and pressed the send button. Her fingers trembled. She held her wrist tightly with the other hand and gave it a nice squeeze. But the trembling persisted. The side of her lips was between her teeth, now sore with all the chewing. Out of pain, she released the lips. She needed something to hang on to, some support to get over this wave. Four or five days, she had to fight her demons. She wanted to rush to Sudha and cry out. It was getting too much for her.

***

The traffic was heavy. It seemed that the entire city was out on the road. Blaring horns, the sound of an assortment of engines, the exhausts spewing carbon monoxide. The insistent beggar knocked at her window with a coin. She did not have the energy to even get upset. She sat in the driver's seat, windows rolled up, tears streaming down endlessly. Her cheeks felt cold, her make-up caked and plastered. Her sobs grew into howls, louder as she banged her clenched fists on the steering wheel. The beggar stared at her and then cleaned his dirty hands on the window before running away to the next car. Commuters watched her with varied reactions—inquisitiveness, suspicion, pity and some as an opportunity. Her howls kept on getting louder as the car snaked amidst a million tail lights. With a limp body, bruised soul and a shattered self, she felt so worthless. What was she? A mother, a worker, a friend, a daughter or just a….

The mere thought made her cringe with repulsion. Why did she have to give in to her demons again? Why couldn't she fight it today the way she had fought them for the last five days? Why did she have to lose it again and get back to the starting block? With every passing red light, the deluge surrounded her more and more.

"Sorry doc, I failed you again." She lamented hoarsely.

***

Ding dong

Ding dong

Ding dong

She kept hitting the doorbell with a vengeance.

"Mommy, I scored an A plus today. Now can we go to McDee this Sunday please?" Tuktuk was exuberant.

Maya dragged herself to her room, dropped her bags

on the floor, shut the door, threw the keys and flung herself on the bed.

As she lay there, looking at the ceiling fan, the images of the evening kept haunting her. She approaching the cab drivers, shamelessly blinded by her craving, in the basement parking of her office, proposing them to have sex with her in the car parked towards the end of the parking, one after another. Living her addiction, her craving, and her impulse.

Who was she? Maya, the woman, the lady, the mother, the boss, the friend, the colleague, or Maya, the sex-addict?

The Dream Chaser

Bad dreams have a wicked habit of leaving one all worked up, scared and restless. Lokesh was no exception. Sitting on the stairs, since early morning, he just watched the street in front of him. But for an occasional passing car, an auto rickshaw or bike, the morning stillness ruled supreme. He turned around and to his right, on the wall, there was a huge poster of the film, which was getting released today. Being a multi-starrer it was supposed to do good business. Splashed with bright colors, posters of the good-looking heroes, gorgeous heroines and scenes from the movies made it such a magnetic sight. To Lokesh, films and their posters were the most beautiful creation of man. He was lost in the poster. But then flashes from the last night's nightmare pulled him back to the vortex of the present.

His feet drummed continually as restlessness was overtaking him. Unfortunately, he had no way of knowing the time. He got up and walked towards the street. The cinema hall, Rachna Talkies, was adjacent to Guru Gobind Street; and could be seen right from the main street, joined by a service road. Situated in the middle of a busy shopping area, on both the sides, it was flanked by shops and restaurants.

As he walked towards the main street, on the pavement, some newspaper hawkers could be seen. They were engrossed in stuffing pamphlets into the folds of the newspapers, arranging their bundles and stacks as per their delivery route map.

"What time is it?"

The question was not aimed at anyone in particular, therefore no one bothered to reply. He kept standing there, waiting for a response.

"What time is it?" He repeated himself again.

Either the hawkers were too absorbed to respond or ignored him like an invisible devil. For a young boy of twelve years, he looked younger due to his undernourished frame. Wearing a long shirt and a pair of fake Nike track pants, he looked something above a street urchin and way below anything respectable. Frustrated at not getting a response, he turned and walked towards the cinema hall building.

He looked at the building. It was quite magnificent.

With its two tone color scheme—beige and brick color, it looked spectacular to him. On the front wall, right there in the middle, there was a huge poster of the film, which was due to be released today. Films fascinated him as they were the only source of existence; literally. He was one of the boys who sold cinema tickets in black at the cinema hall. The modus operandi was simple—come early and buy tickets in blocks and when people turned up for the show, many of them found the 'house full' board challenging them. To beat the same, they were ready to pay any price. This was the juncture in the plot where Lokesh slipped in; offering them a solution by waving tickets; at double or three times the price of the original one. During a hit movie, he would do good business. Even after paying the cut to the local cops, the area goons, his earnings were sufficient to take care of his needs.

The newspaper hawkers left on their cycles. He looked at the poster again. His instincts told him that this movie would be a big hit. For the same reason, his last night's nightmare scared him more. It flashed before his eyes again and he had to close them tight and open again, to get rid of the scene. He shuddered at the thought of his nightmare coming true. Last night, after he woke up, drenched in sweat, panting, his initial reaction was to shrug off his nightmare as another dream. But he had been doing the same for the past four days. And the day had come when he had either to act upon his instincts or let his worst nightmare come true. He chose the earlier option.

***

The tea shack at the end of the service lane had opened up. He walked towards it. The owner, Bhola, knew him well.

"*Ram-Ram*." He greeted Bhola.

"*Ram-Ram*, Lokesh. How come today you are here so early?"

Before Lokesh could respond, the answer also came his way, "I see, it seems you want to buy all the tickets to make big money." Bhola laughed at his wit.

Lokesh did not know what to say. Yes, he wanted to buy all the tickets. He was there for the same. However, the reason for buying all the tickets was different.

***

"*Chacha*, please, I will pay you the money."

"Don't be crazy. Firstly, I can't sell you all the tickets, secondly, definitely not on credit and thirdly, stop chewing off my brains right in the morning."

"*Chacha*, please. I beg of you, please."

"*Saale*, have you lost it? I have to deposit cash after lunch. I can't take any chances. You will disappear and I will get fired."

"Trust me *Chacha*, I will repay you, every single penny."

"You know I like you. But that doesn't mean that I would lose my mind. Get away from the counter now."

Lokesh was disappointed. How painstakingly he had made a foolproof plan to do what he intended to without letting anyone ridicule him. He knew that if he shared the original reason for buying all the tickets, people would scoff at him. But now it seemed that his carefully crafted, foolproof plan was not working.

"What if I get the money? Would you let me have all the tickets for the night show?" He pleaded.

"Have you gone out of your mind? I can't give you all the tickets."

"Please do me this favor. Please."

"Are you even aware how much money it will take to book the entire hall for the night show?"

"How much?" Lokesh had no clue about the exact amount but he knew that it would cost a fortune.

"160 second class tickets, 140 first class tickets and 220 seats in the balcony. Multiply them by 10, 15 and 25." Inept at handling so many numbers at one go, he just stood there.

"Please *Chacha*." He beseeched again.

"Ok, go and get the money," he blurted. At least it would give him some peace of mind and riddance from this early morning nuisance.

"Thank you. I will go and get the money." Lokesh ran towards his destiny.

***

"*Amma*, I need money."

"You scoundrel, how many times you have borrowed from me, assuring that you would return it? Have you ever done so? Don't you ask me for any more now."

Watching her, standing bare feet in an old cotton sari, which had seen more summers than it deserved, he knew that his mom had a reason to be annoyed. Working as a part-time maid during morning time and then a half-day maid for the rest of the day, she worked tirelessly to fuel the liquor addiction of her husband. Lokesh had stopped acknowledging the man as his father long back. Now his drunken brawls and incessant quarrels didn't matter anymore.

"*Amma*, don't say no. I know you have lots of money stashed away somewhere."

He implored knowing that it was impossible to take money from his mother, certainly not for any scheme.

"Why not? I have hit a jackpot and have tucked away millions in this make-shift, trampoline covered home."

"You would repent if you don't give me money this time." The scheme was being unfurled.

"As if you are going to double it in one month." She

pushed Lokesh away.

"Not in a month, but fifteen days." He smiled.

With great difficulty he had calculated that to buy all the tickets for the night show, he required eight to ten thousand rupees. Arranging such a large sum was impossible. Still he was hopeful. Only if he had some time, he knew he could have done it.

"*Amma*, don't think, it's time to act. Now or never offer." He teased her.

"I am not falling into that trap, you rascal. Get away from here."

"*Amma*, you will repent. I mean it."

"Let me complete my chores and you better run off. I don't have any money."

His plan was falling apart. He could not let it slip away.

'Stop being a miser. I am your son. Can't you trust me?" Business proposition turned into emotional blackmail.

"No, I can't. Just get away from here." She wiped her brow, which already had sweat due to the heat from the stove.

He got agitated, as he knew if someone else reached the ticket counter, the tickets would be gone. He had to collect eight thousand rupees and that too, fast.

***

"Salim, I need my money."

"How much?"

"All of it."

"And you think that I am sitting here on your money, eh?"

"Salim, I want it now." Lokesh was getting furious. After all he was asking for his own money which he kept on investing in a chit fund being run by the local mutton shop owner, Salim.

"Lokesh, what is wrong with you?"

"Salim, I'm in no mood to argue. I want it now."

"See, you know that I invest the money to give you better return. You also know that your money is safe. Then why this haste?"

"I need the money for something important, very important." He appealed.

"Hope you are not buying a necklace for your new found love, that slut, Rajjo." Salim guffawed. Lokesh ignored the snide remark as he was in no mood to get into any kind of altercation and lose the track.

"Ok, if you don't have my money, can you lend me eight thousand rupees?"

"What?" Salim almost fell off the wooden block he was sitting on, chopping the thigh off the lamb.

"Yes, I need eight thousand."

"You have gone crazy."

"No, I have not. But I need the money."

"Lokesh, don't waste my time. Go away." He got back

to the thigh of the lamb.

"I'm not kidding and I'm asking for my money." The voice was stern.

"Lower that voice kid. Firstly, I don't owe you anything and secondly, even if I were to return your money, it won't be more than four or five hundred rupees."

"You are lying."

"You bastard, how dare you call me a liar?" Salim got up and grabbed Lokesh by his collar.

"I want my money." Lokesh gripped Salim's wrist and tried setting himself free.

Salim pushed him away and Lokesh landed on the footpath. Salim put his hand under the sheet of jute bag he was sitting on, pulling out some money.

"You have paid me fifty rupees for eight months. As you are taking money out of turn, here are your three hundred rupees. And don't forget to pay the rest or else instead of this leg piece it will be yours." Salim threw the blood and flesh grimed currency at him. Lokesh grabbed the notes, counted them and got up. He wanted to kill Salim but then he was running out of time.

"You son of a bitch, wait till I come back to get you." Lokesh sprinted away before Salim could even change his expression.

***

He knew that the ticket counter would have opened by now. He also knew that the elderly man; the ticket seller whom he fondly addressed as *Chacha* would surely wait for him. For how long, that was the question.

***

"Lukkha, I need eight thousand rupees."

"Tell me the number of zeros and you shall have it."

"Please."

"Fuck off you bastard. Go slow on the weed. It will kill you."

"I'm not high. Please give me the money."

"Send your mom. In any case that drunkard father of yours won't be doing her, let me make her happy. Maybe I will give you two hundred?"

"You mother fucker. Send your sister to me. I will give you three hundred." Lokesh waved the money at him and ran away.

***

"Number *paanch*." Lokesh put the ten-rupee note on number five which was printed on a black sheet of paper. The paper had a grid with various numbers.

The man sitting there put two dice in a glass, and shook the glass vigorously. As he rolled the dice, Lokesh prayed. He wanted to win at any cost. The dice rotated and stopped at three and four. He wanted to take another chance.

"Number *chaar*." He mumbled again and put a ten-rupee note on number four.

Number five, and six and seven, he went on. With every loss he got more desperate to win, ending up losing more. Before he could realise it, he had lost one hundred rupees. Left with two hundred rupees, he walked out of the small makeshift room, which could have let him earn five times the amount he had. Too bad, not his day. The sun was high and he felt like a loser.

Should he snatch a chain or someone's purse? But what if he got caught? Not that he was afraid of the cops but that would deter his plan of buying the tickets for the night show. He was in no position to let that happen.

***

After all the begging, pleading, cajoling and hoodwinking, he could only collect three hundred and sixteen rupees. And that money could get him ten tickets of balcony and four of first class. Only fourteen tickets in total! With tears in his eyes, he kept looking at the tickets, feeling sorry for himself, cursing God and just about anyone and everyone. He knew that the night was going to be a long one. He thought of going to the cinema hall but then decided against it. He had tried his best, he still had fourteen tickets. Too bad there were four hundred more to go.

Looking at the tickets, praying hard, tired after the long day, he dozed off. Fortunately for him, that night the nightmare did not occur.

***

"Fire Tragedy at Rachna Cinema. 59 people dead and more than hundred seriously injured."

As every newspaper described the tragedy during the night show at Rachna Cinema in great detail, for Lokesh the dilemma was profound. The joy of saving fourteen lives or the remorse of not being able to save the rest?

ॐ✤ॐ

The Guardian Angel

Thunderous applause greeted the air, which was still heady with the echoes of sweet symphony. He bowed down, acknowledging the love and appreciation of the audience. The applause was getting bigger. He lived only for these few seconds as it were these moments, which made his life worthwhile. Today he was playing for the German Ambassador who was visiting the restaurant. He had specially sent in a request that he would like to listen to some Beethoven.

The performance was over and life had to move back to its basics. He got off the stage and walked towards the chair kept just adjacent to the stage. The steps were precisely calculated and he had no hassle in following the same. He placed himself on the comfortable chair and took a sigh of relief. Today was an important day. The General Manager of the hotel had requested him to be at his best as the client was important for the hotel.

"Sharat, some water?"

The sweetheart that Bennet was, like everyday he was there with his request.

"What would I do without you, Bennet?" Sharat smiled.

"You don't have to do without me." He handed him the glass.

Sharat emptied the lifeline in one large gulp. He never realized how thirsty he was. "Thank you Bennet."

"Stop thanking me every day for smallest of the things." His anger was laced with deep love and affection.

"I'm sorry, I can't help but thank God and the people around me. Life has been so kind to me."

"You know Sharat, it is this gratitude of yours which makes me come to you every time. I mean, in your place had there been anyone else, he would have cursed everything, everyone around. But look at you, so much at peace with yourself, your being and the environment. You are a saint."

"Ask the priest of your church to recommend my name for sainthood. I would love being addressed as Saint Sharat Kumar." Sharat laughed and Bennet joined him.

"Come, let me escort you till the bus stop."

"Don't bother yourself. I can make it on my own."

"What if I insist?"

"Then like every other day, I will have to concede."

"Give me a minute." Bennet got back on the stage and placed the violin and the bow in the hard shell case. Sharat got up from the chair and flipped his wrist to open his white walking stick.

"Bennet, do you see that woman today also?" Sharat whispered.

"Remember, yesterday you had warned me never to bring her up during our conversation?"Bennet reminded him of the vow.

"Come on, I am just asking you. You can say a yes or no."

"Yes."

"What yes."

"You only asked me to respond with a yes or a no. So I said yes. It means that she is here."

"Where is she?"

"Till a few minutes back, she was sitting in the last row, watching you intently."

"Hmmm."

"And you know, today she was dressed for the occasion. Nice, wine-toned, heavy silk *saree*, white pearls around her neck, matching earrings. She looked prettier. It seems that she knew that today was a special day for you and to match the occasion she also had dressed accordingly."

"Hmmm."Sharat looked around as if trying to find her amidst all the darkness that surrounded him.

"What hmmm? Why don't you have a word with her? At least ask her who she is? Don't you feel like knowing why she has been coming with you daily for all these years? I mean if I were you, I would have freaked out. In today's world, there is hardly any time. Then why is this lady following you? You are no Ranbir Kapoor."

Both laughed. They got off the elevator and started walking in the lobby, towards the door, that led to the porch of the hotel.

"You know Bennet, we all have our Guardian Angels. They differ in forms and shapes, but everyone has got one. They are with you, guarding you. They never speak, touch or even present themselves till there is a dire need."

"But then why can't I see mine?"

"Because you can see the world around you. So your guardian angel would be cleverly camouflaged. For a blind man like me, there is no need for him or her to hide, as I can't see in any case." Sharat smiled.

"Twenty-eight, twenty-nine and there should be the handle of the exit door." He extended his left hand.

"When I'm with you then why do you need to count your steps?"

"Bennet, no offence, but for me closed eyes is a permanent feature. And to overcome it, I can't depend on anyone but my own self. I have you here, with me. But what would I do when I get out of this hotel? If I get complacent, it will creep into my system, and for a blind man like me, it can lead to disaster."

***

"Here you are." The conductor took his hand and guided him to a vacant seat. "It seems that today you had a special show."

"Why do you ask?"

"Your fan is dressed big time."

"Shhh, don't embarrass her. And look at me while you talk, not towards her."

"How on earth did you know that I was not looking at you?"

"Simple, the voice was travelling away from me, not coming towards me, implying that the source of the voice was turned away from me."

"You should have been a detective, not a musician." They laughed.

"Is the bus crowded today?"

"Not really, but she is sitting at her designated place, reading a book."

"Hmmm."

"Can I ask you something?" The conductor's voice was soft and curious.

"Don't you ever feel like talking to her, asking her who is she, why does she follow you, what is her interest in you?"

"Remember what I told you the other day?"

"Yeah, some mumbo-jumbo about guardian angels and how they leave you if they get a whiff that you know about them."

"You are a smart man." Sharat smiled.

"And you are like no other I have ever met. At least ask her name?"

"Why can't you just get back to punching your tickets?" He chided him playfully.

"You lucky man." The bus conductor mumbled.

"That I can see." He responded playfully.

He touched the dial of his watch. Another five minutes and he would be home. His stomach was rumbling. What would be there for dinner? He wanted to keep his mind busy as for some reason, today, it was going back to his fan, stalker or whom he referred to as a guardian angel. He was feeling tempted to have a word with her. He had no clue for how long she had been following him. Her presence was only revealed when Bennet told him about her some two years back. Then out of sheer curiosity, he enquired from the bus conductor too. He also corroborated Bennet's story.

***

Tic, toc, tic, toc, tic, toc, tic, toc…

Sharat could clearly hear a pair of heels, in a great hurry, following him. An upsurge of fear overtook him. Today was not the usual sound of muted footsteps that accompanied him. The sudden change at this hour was scaring him. Though he could not check time but he knew that it would be close to 10:30 pm. The stillness of the surroundings told him that nothing much was happening around him. What should he do? Should he call out for help? His mind advised him against his initial thought. Firstly, he should be sure of the fact if the lady in heels was following him. Slow down your speed, he told himself. Gradually, he decreased his speed.

Tic, toc, tic, toc, tic, toc… the speed picked up and kept on getting closer.

He started sweating.

The echo of heels kept on getting closer and closer.

His heartbeat was pounding like a bass drum.

The walking stick had a visible tremble.

Close and closer and then the sound of the heels crossed him and went ahead.

He stopped, as he wanted to be sure that the scary sound of the heels had overtaken him. The reverberation of heels on the cobbled pathway was clearly moving away. He took out his handkerchief and wiped his face. The encounter was too close for his comfort.

***

"The show went off very well." Sharat placed the violin case on the centre table and made his way towards the dining table.

"See, I told you that it would. I know my son is super talented."

"Come on mom, you are being kind."

"No, I mean it."

He pulled a dining chair and sat down.

"Mom, what's for dinner?"

"Your favorite; grilled sandwich, soup and baked veggies."

"Wow, I'm so hungry."

"Coming to you in less than ten seconds."

"You know what mom…"

Tic, toc, tic, toc, tic, toc

"Your soup is here. Start with it and I will get the sandwich and the veggies too."

Tic, toc, tic, toc, the footsteps walked towards the kitchen.

After all, who could be a better guardian angel than a mother?

രുംഷ

Every Mouse Ain't
A Mickey Mouse

"Another drink please," I gestured.

I was already three drinks down. Considering my mental state, age and the fact that I had to drive, another one could prove to be fatal. But then who cared? Today was the day, the only day, as there was no tomorrow. I was on a course that promised the liberation of the mind and soul.

The young waiter placed my drink on the large oak table. It gleamed with all the care it was subjected to everyday. Though the same could not be said for the waiter's face. Behind his tutored and plastic smile, strong undercurrents of turbulence were clearly visible. I could empathize with his turmoil. I shared it too—the turmoil of scuttling in life, the one of being a rat. Aren't we all rats? Well, the level of acceptance could vary but nevertheless the fact would be irrefutable, standing like a monolith in the middle of the small courtyard of life.

It was another day, mundane and humid. Since morning I was feeling low. There were no apparent reasons. Surely, chancing upon a rat, right in the middle of the road, on my way to the office, couldn't have been the reason.

Like any other day, I had left early for work. Early start made me avoid the morning traffic rush and also gave some spare time to sort out my official e-mails etc. Today morning as I hit the relatively empty stretch of road and stepped on the accelerator, right there in the middle of the road, I saw something move. Maybe a cloth or a newspaper, I told myself. As I got closer, I strained my eyes. The newspaper thing was crawling and had a pronounced tail. Owing to my speed, in no time I got closer to the object and realized it was a rat. A fat, grey, wet rodent, scurrying for shelter. Too bad on that road there was none. I sharply steered towards my right and went past it. But for some unknown reason, the image stuck to my mind.

During the course of my day I kept on wondering about the fate of that rat. Would it be still safe? Early morning traffic was sparse and its chances of making it to the end of the road were high. I cursed myself for not stopping by and helping the poor thing. I chided myself for being selfish and not helping a life form when I could have. The guilt of leaving the rat right there in the middle of the street was distressing me. I had no idea why I felt so sympathetic towards the rat? I had no reason…

…Or did I? Wasn't feeling for one of my kind natural? After all, I am a rat; we are all rats. That is what this rat race makes us. Running mindlessly, without even stopping for a moment to think what makes us run, what would we achieve, what destination we have on our minds? Just to avoid the rat behind us from getting ahead, we run with all our might. Panting hard, yet running. Our lungs ready to burst, legs unable to carry the burden of our greed, heart doing its best by pumping more and more to meet our mindless ambition. But we run, with a mind that is dead, or at the best, sloshed.

***

"Jay, let us meet at two in the conference room for our review meeting."

"Sure Mr Rat, why not." I mumbled.

As I looked around, I could see the entire office infested with rats. Big ones, small ones, cute ones, sexy ones, fat ones, ugly ones, but nevertheless, all rats. Rats running to the Xerox machine, the coffee machine, to the admin or the accounts department. Rats with headphones trying to assuage hyper clients, typing feverishly, gossiping about their boss rats and bitch rats. Was my mind playing up?

I rubbed my eyes. Yeah, they were humans but as good as the rat I had seen in the morning—dragging itself, tired and pitiable. I felt my face. The skin was sagging. I ran my fingers through my hair—thin and lacklustre. Couldn't help but hurry towards the washroom. Standing there, in front of the mirror, I checked my face. It looked haggard with a crisscross of fine lines firmly etched on it. The receding hairline was moving faster than the legendary sprinter, Ben Johnson. The puffy dark circles were showing no sign of improvement despite the regular use of the expensive under-eye cream. Black spots were making a comeback. I could see an ageing rat, fighting hard.

I pulled in my tummy and came out, feeling miserable. Maybe I needed some pep in my life. After all, we were all rats; I consoled myself. I knew that we chose this race, as there was no choice, or so we were told. We were meant to go to school, top our class, join medicine or engineering. For the lesser mortals, it was some top ranked college, which paved the way forward to the IIMs and then to some MNC bank or a soft drink company. And the rat race was far from getting over. We were supposed to choose a fellow rat, find a great looking hole, settle down and breed more rats. After all, the race should go on. And to make it exciting, there ought to be more and more rats, at every level.

Was there any difference between a rat and a mouse? This sudden question, which my inner self popped, confused me. I never assumed that there would be any as I kept on using the words interchangeably. Rat v/s Mouse. I typed the Google URL but was repulsed at the thought of my dependence. No wonder, I was a rodent. What difference would it make if both were the same or even different? Would it improve my state of mind or sense of feeling? Would it take care of my sagging skin, dark circles and coarse hair?

"Sir, I was wondering if you have reviewed the deck I had sent you yesterday." A sweet voice interrupted the confusion around rats, mice and rodents.

She was a pretty young rat. Or would her type make her a mouse? Mouse sounded cute, or so I thought. Damn, I shrugged my shoulders. I got my focus back on the mouse in front of me. In her twenties, some day she would breed more of her kind with some lucky son-of-a-bitch, I meant lucky son of a mouse. How would she be in bed? How are mice in bed, but they don't really go to bed, do they? Gosh, I was getting carried away. I scanned her and my eyes liked her creamy and soft skin. I would love to mate with her, like crazy. Why do they look so desirable when they are young and get progressively disgusting as they turn older? How would I mate with this mouse? Would I take her to one of the fancy hotels and pin her down? So clichéd! I parked the hotel room fantasy on one side. What if I took her scuba diving and do her underwater? Wow, I got excited at the proposition. In this nerve-wracking rat race, I had lost the power to think beyond the conventional, stereotype positions. But what was making me the rebel now?

"Give me some time, please." The rat in me, with a hard-on, squeaked.

As she walked out of my cabin, I stared at her derrière, scanning for the tell-tale signs of a tail. I wondered why we hated lust so much? Why was it kept under wraps? Was it any sin to experience lust? I could think of my life, which was dotted with the use of the word 'love'. Was I even aware of its meaning when I said it for the first time or the second or for that matter even the last time? What was love? A convenient and guaranteed form of receiving conditional care and attention, a garb to get in bed and fuck each other officially?

Are rats predisposed to love or are they driven by lust? Do they breed out of love or lust? Did I breed out of lust or love? My two children were a product of lust or love? If my lovemaking had no lust how would I have consummated? Was lust a part of love? The rat in me got confused.

"Jay, the market share has been shrinking over the past two quarters."

Damn, the corporate rat race had started. Here all the rats run for the inanimate rat, the corporate. These corporates were the prime reason of this rat race. Everyone wanted to be the fattest rat sitting at the top, enjoying the most comfortable chair. Too bad, the rats never realise that there was none. When I was a trainee, I assumed that the chair of an Assistant Manager would be comfy. Now even as the Vice President, I was still a rat. And rats are meant to run, not to seek comfort.

Amidst soaring dreams and ambitions, the hunger to have more, showing-off to relatives and friends, living under the constant threat of pink slip, paying EMIs, saving for son and daughter, managing pension and health plans, now I could see life only in the rear view mirror.

Another day of rat race at work got over. Another day of non-performance! At this rate, the bunch of rats just behind me would trample me. I was in no situation to lose my job, my position. I just couldn't. It defined who I was. Jay Sharma, Vice President, Xanders Technologies. Sounds super cool and is self explanatory of my intellect and hard work. I shudder at the thought of being Jay Sharma, just Jay Sharma. I would have so much of explanation to do to prove my efficiency, if someday the suffix, 'Vice President' was deleted.

'Jay Sharma, Vice President, come on, get up, you need a drink.'

***

"Excuse me." The waiter knew what I wanted and in no time got me another re-fill of my staple liquid diet; Glenfiddich; large with two cubes of ice.

"Is this my fifth one?" I didn't fail to notice the effort I had to make to raise my head and ask the question.

"Sir, sixth."

No wonder I was feeling so liberated.

A liberated rat? Yes, wish all the rats could be soaked in a barrel of Glenfiddich. There would be no desire, dream, ego, hunger, greed, no place to go, no race and the world would be such a saner place.

When was the last time when I expressed myself in front of my CEO? When was the last time when I spoke to my wife honestly, telling her that life had no meaning with her as our marriage had failed? When was the last time when I told my children that I would not be their ATM any more? If they thought they were grown-up to do their own things—search, and choose their life partners, set up their own places in Cardiff and New York respectively, then they ought to be self-respecting enough to stop asking money from me. When was the last time when I told my brother how much I miss the time when we played cricket?

Why can't I tell him that he has no reason to be jealous of my success, as I am his own brother? Why can't I send money to my mom and sister without hiding it from my wife? After all, it is my money. I have the right to spend it anywhere I please. And more so, I had responsibilities towards my mother and widowed sister too.

Why do I have to be a part of the Golf Club circuit when I don't enjoy it? Why do I have to read the discolored *Economic Times* when my heart wants to enjoy *Tintin*? Why do I have to look sombre and in control when I want to be the lost one, without any notion of time, place or destination?

"Sir, we are closing for the day."

"Can I have another large, last one?"

Tomorrow I will gain my lost ground—my expression, life, dream, lust, honesty, pride, religion, grounding and roots. Shit, this rat race has made me lose everything I had or was blessed with. I had no clue when I stopped being the son to my father and mother, brother to my brother and sister, uncle to my nieces and nephews. I could not think why and how the word 'my family' started implying my wife and my kids. I tried hard thinking of the time when sports got replaced with games, honesty with sanity, expression with statements and life with success.

What if I achieved everything that I ever wanted? What if I never achieved anything that I wanted? Who would hail me once I would be gone? I would just be a picture on a wall or a RIP message on someone's Facebook status.

Never too late! I will set things right. Tomorrow first thing in the morning, I would send in my resignation. Better if I call up my boss and ask him to get lost.

I loved the thought of me firing my boss. Yes, I would do it. I smiled, after very long. Second thing, I would tell my wife to have the apartment, the bank balance, the FDs, the cars, everything and to set me free. Third, I would call up my kids and tell them to stop treating me as their bank. And then I would pack my bags and leave. With no destination on my mind, I would be the true traveller. I would see, I would sing, I would celebrate, I would dance, I would fall in love, I would experience lust, I would rejoice life and I would live.

I stopped my car, as my bladder was unable to hold the drinks any longer. Freedom, here I come.

***

Lying there in the middle of the road, in a pool of blood, hurled several feet away from my car, by a speeding truck, I tried to move, but my limbs failed to respond. Maybe a broken bone. I tried to wriggle my toe. No reaction. I tried getting up but it seemed that but for my head, I did not have a body. Why didn't I feel any pain, not even a thing? I ought to be fine. Come on, move yourself off the road. Get in your car and drive away. Tomorrow is your day. Reclaim your life, your freedom. Come on Jay, you rodent, you bloody rat, get up.

I couldn't move a millimetre. Where was my phone? I tried reaching for my pocket but my hands failed to respond. What was wrong? Why couldn't I move? Did too many drinks make me feel so light? How could there be blood and no pain?

The rat lay there, silently, waiting for another Jay either to steer away or run over him.

ରେ ❖ ୨୦

Smart TV

"Sheela, come downstairs. Please get Neha too." Raj sounded buoyant.

"I am busy and Neha is studying." A very wife-like response came from the other end of the line.

"What nonsense? Why can't both of you come for five minutes?" He sounded annoyed.

"In middle of cooking. Don't want you to create any scene just because your dinner wasn't ready on time."

In no time Raj realized that his anger was the reason for holding his wife back. "Come on darling, dinner can wait. And if you want, we can order food from outside. What do you say?" He adjusted his phone closer to his ear.

"Please, I don't want to eat those roadside *chane-bhature*. I'd rather cook."

The last line infuriated Raj. "What do you mean by roadside? Haven't I taken you to fancy restaurants? Didn't we go to Taj the other day?"

"Yeah, we did. You were attending some conference and you made us join and have dinner there, with your office colleagues and other delegates. It was so embarrassing. Listen, I'm keeping down the phone. Can't talk."

"Why do you have to be self-conscious of everything? Did anyone say anything?"

Raj was there, obstinately guarding his stance.

"Raj, I don't like going with you to your formal office parties. I mean, if we are invited, if your other colleagues are getting their spouses along then it is fine, but getting there un-invited, it is so awkward."

"My colleagues are assholes. Can I help if they don't love their families?" The conversation was going on a different tangent.

"I really appreciate that bit of you. But you know even if it were a small outing, a decent restaurant, I would love to go with you and Neha and spend some quality time. But I really don't enjoy gatecrashing your office parties. I am sure they all would be making fun of you."

"I don't know why you need to have an opinion on everything and more so when it is not even justified." He snapped.

"Sorry, I will play the dumb wife. Bye."

"Now what is this? I can't even express myself?" Raj retraced his steps.

"That was humiliation, not expression."

"Ok sweetie pie, why are we doing this on the phone? My apologies, now please come down with Neha. Please." He pleaded.

"Do you think I'm a robot programmed to follow your instruction, irrespective of time and my mood?"

"Ok, don't come. There is no point in doing anything for you guys. You should be just left there to rot." He went back to his original, sarcastic self and flicked the button to disconnect the call.

"Sir, please move your car. It is blocking the gate." The guard requested.

"You are just a guard and in your own interest act like one." Even the polite request of the guard further provoked Raj.

"That is what I am doing. Move your car to your parking." Curtness elicited more of it.

"What if I don't?" In no time ego-trip came into play.

"In that case I will call the supervisor who will come and clamp your wheels. Also, the RWA will issue you a warning." The guard was being factual.

"You bastard, how dare you?" Raj got off the car, rolling up his sleeves.

"Mind your language. I am just doing my duty. You are not supposed to park your car here." The guard pulled out his baton, ready to hit at any further provocation.

"You wretched scum, you are here to serve, not order." Raj screamed.

"You've got it wrong. I am here to serve the residents and not be your servant. You don't pay my salary, the RWA does."

"You mother-fucker, we pay you, and don't you bark at me."

"If you don't behave, I won't mind biting you too."

Suddenly the elevator door opened and a middle-aged lady walked out, wearing a blue *salwar-suit*.

"Madam, see how your husband is behaving." The guard complained.

"Don't you get her in between our conversation, you creep."

"Raj, what is wrong? Why are you howling?" The lady admonished him.

"Madam, he has been abusing me, calling me a dog, bastard and what not."

"Thank your lucky stars that I did not bash you."

"Raj, please behave, this is so embarrassing."

"Why don't you teach him some manners too?" The guard was in no mood of letting the issue go.

"*Bhaiya,* I'm sorry. Please don't mind what he has said."

"Now my wife is going to apologize to a guard earning

five thousand rupees. *Bhaiya*, my foot!" Raj was fuming.

"Had it not been for the respect we have for Madam, I would have slapped you." The guard looked at Raj, directly threatening him.

"Raj, please stop this. Please. Why were you calling me? Tell me Raj, please." The lady tried taking him off the heated course.

***

"Wow, that's a nice TV."

"This is why I was calling you and Neha downstairs."

"Why did you have to buy such an expensive TV when we already have one?" Sheela complained lovingly.

"Star sales performers don't buy anything, people gift them." His hands on the hips, the patent grin flashed, which was between a smile and a smirk.

"*Paapu*, you are my real superman. Who gifted you this?" Neha was all excited.

"My boss. I completed my second quarter target in just two months."

"Congrats *Paapu*. I am so proud of you." Neha hugged him tight. She still had traces of Electra complex.

"And mind you, this is no ordinary TV. It's a Smart TV."

"Come on, a TV is a TV." Sheela played the content housewife.

"Darling, why don't you tell your mommy that in smart

age, everything has to be smart—phone, TV and now even wives." Raj looked at Neha and winked. They both laughed. Of course, Sheela did not appreciate the pun.

"Ok, I am dumb. But I insist that a TV is still a TV. Can it help me in the kitchen?"

"Oh God, Sheela, why does your life have to revolve around the kitchen?" He gave an exasperated look.

"Because, if it doesn't, you won't be getting your morning tea and breakfast, two vegetables, rice, *chapati, dal,* curd and salad for lunch and again a full course dinner."

"Jesus, this is for seventy-five thousand!" Neha, who was inspecting the box, exclaimed.

"What?" It was Sheela's turn now. "Why didn't you ask your boss to give you cash instead? We could have done a fixed deposit with the same. Seventy-five thousand on a TV? What a waste!"

"Darling, please tell your mom that life is meant to be lived king size, especially when her husband is the Sales Star of Sunrise Enterprise." Raj flashed his patent grin again.

"Raj, please grow up. You are not getting any younger and we have to plan for Neha's future too. Do I have to remind you that there has been no sales incentive for whole of the last year? Now that you got in this quarter, you come home with a TV. It is getting impossible to run this house with your salary."

"Sheela, why do you always have to be a spoilsport?"

Raj shot back.

"I am not complaining, but you have to wake up to the reality. Youngsters who were hired by you have been promoted and now are at your level. They are making more money than you are. I don't want to pull you down but then I can't lead you down the blind alley either."

"Mom, please. My *Paapu* is the best." Neha hugged him again.

"You and your *Paapu*." She walked away in disgust.

"Neha, come help me in installing this smart one. Then we can sit and watch it together."

"Yes *Paapu*, smart you and smart me." She beamed with joy.

'Come here," he whispered, signaling Neha to come to him. Neha smiled and walked towards him. He put his lips close to her ears and whispered, "Smart *paapu*, smart daughter but dumb mommy." They both burst out laughing.

***

"Tell your Papa that Mahabharata is about to start or else he will be sulking till the next day." Sheela instructed Neha.

"*Paapu*, Mahabharata is about to start." Neha shrieked as she fidgeted with the remote.

"*Beta*, five minutes. Let me have a shower."

"Mom, this TV looks so cool. Ain't it?"

Sheela stared at her. Neha got the hint.

"What Mom, I will study after this serial. Promise."

"*Beta*, it is your smartness and hard work which will help you, not this smart TV."

"Why are you always so negative?" Her eyes were glued to the remote, as she was trying to figure it out.

"Because as your mother I am worried for you."

"*Paapu* never scolds me, you always do."

"Neha, I'm not your enemy. "

Suddenly the TV screen, which was playing advertisements, went blank and turned deep blue.

'Searching for Bluetooth devices,' the line on the screen read.

'Connecting Raj Sales Star' it blinked again.

And a chat box opened.

DashingDude: A promise is a promise

Both Neha and Sheela were shocked and surprised. They could not figure out the sudden jump.

Jasmine: You always make them

DashingDude: Do you doubt me?

Jasmine: I have reasons

Sheela looked towards Neha with utter dismay.

DashingDude: This time I'm taking my baby to Kerala. Three nights-four days at a five star hotel.

Jasmine: Wow! When?

DashingDude: Next week, tickets and hotel have been done.

Jasmine: But I mean how come all of a sudden?

DashingDude: When you have a sales star as your boy friend, you should be ready to live life king size.

Jasmine: Oh baby, I love you so much.

DashingDude: Keep loving me or someone else will.

Jasmine: You horny bastard, I love you so much.

DashingDude: Love you baby.

Jasmine: Won't your family complain?

DashingDude: Have given them a TV to keep them happy. And who would go to Kerala with that old cow? She is just fit to be a maid.

Jasmine: You naughty, mean man, love you.

Teardrops trickled down from two pairs of appalled and hurt eyes.

ରୁ❖ରୁ

True Lies

"Father, I have a confession to make." The voice was tense and highly strung. All these years of experience had given the Father an uncanny ability of mapping voices and matching them with the personality of the confessor. It was a sin to look at the confessor, but profiling him or her did not breach any textbook rule.

The Father pulled himself up on the chair and sat straight. Involuntarily he fixed the pleats of his cassock. Goa in June was bad—hot, humid and sultry. Though the high ceiling of the main hall was some protection, but the high beams from which the fans hung, did little to combat the humid onslaught.

"Yes my child, I'm listening. Whatever you say will be a secret between the Lord and you. The generous Lord shall forgive you for any sin which you might have committed intentionally or unintentionally."

The confessor had especially called for this confession session. The Father had no choice but to accept, as her voice told him that something was seriously wrong and any delay could have disastrous results.

"I am going to commit suicide." The opening line of the girl confirmed his premonition. "And please don't try to dissuade me. I just wanted you to know, or the Lord, or whosoever and move on with my plan." She sounded focused and revengeful.

She ought to be in her twenties, height around 5'4", slightly plump, round face and black eyes, and in all probability hadn't slept the previous night. The Father did a quick profiling. He knew that profiling a confessor always aided him in assisting better.

"My child, taking away something as precious as life is the gravest of the sins one can think of." While his mind was trying to find a solution, he initiated a dialogue, to engage her.

"Father, I have made up my mind and there is nothing which is going to stop me."

The voice was firm and edgy and the tone conveyed her resolve. Father D'Souza knew that people in sticky situations became hopeless, assuming that they were the ones singled out by God. His experience had taught him that settling issues was a long and phased exercise.

"Since you have come here to make a confession, let us start with it. In the house of the Lord, there are no sinners; if they confess and make a resolve not to repeat the sin again." He tried being gentle yet firm.

"Father, at this point in time, I see no hope. I have been responsible for ruining my life. And for me, there is no going back. I don't know how to put it across, but I have become a source of disgrace; both to myself and my family." She paused for a moment. "I am single, out of job, pregnant and my boyfriend does not want to marry me. I shudder to think of the consequences this news will have on my family, especially my mom. She adores me like crazy. I have been a failure and I think in the larger interest, I have to end my wretched life, saving everyone from the barrage of humiliation."

"My child, I am glad you could bring yourself to confess." He tried keeping his tone sympathetic.

"Father, I am already feeling much better and I am sure it has helped me in lessening the quantum of my sin. I won't take much of your time. Forgive me if you can."

He knew that she was about to get up and walk away. During the course of her confession, he could figure out that the girl had committed some blunders, a result of bad choices and decisions. Owing to the same and her inexperience, she was assuming her situation to be irreversible. He wished if he could walk out of the confession chamber and counsel her. But then it was not allowed. Very well, he thought to himself, maybe it was time to seek some divine intervention.

"My child, can I ask for a favor?"

"Is there anything I can still do for anyone?" Her voice was bereft of any hope.

"Certainly. Till our last breath, we all can do something or the other for fellow humans." Sitting inside the confession box, the Father could visualize a glint of hope in her eyes. "I'm not asking for much. As you requested for an early confession, it did upset my schedule. I have some important work to attend to. Can I request you to sit in this confession box and listen to the few confessions which could come your way?"

She was taken aback and did not know how to respond to that strange request.

"Father, are you sure? I mean, do you think I'm sensible enough to listen to confessions?"

"If you are mature enough to decide to end your life, I am sure you can listen to confessions too." His voice was still placid.

"Yes, maybe you are right. And anyway I won't be here much longer. So their confessions can go with me, safe and undisclosed."

"See, how smart you are. You have figured out the logical conclusion too." The Father couldn't help but smile.

He could figure out that the girl also smiled.

"Ok, I am getting out of the box. Please come and be seated in. You need not say anything. People will come, confess and leave. I will join you in the next hour or so."

***

"Father, my heart is riddled with guilt and remorse and I want to confess."

A man's voice shook the girl out of her thoughts. She felt a little embarrassed sitting in the box, pretending to be the real Father. But as she had promised to fill in for him, now she had no alternative. So she cleared her throat to let the man know that someone was in the confession box.

"Father, I ran a small shack and was leading a decent, happy life. After years of prayers, the Lord blessed me with a child. We gave him everything. The best of clothes, toys, school and nutrition. We even gave him things which were beyond our means. Sent him to Mumbai to a reputed college. My relatives, my neighbors were so proud of him. He was a bright kid and was destined for bigger things in life. He was also a God-fearing boy, docile and well-mannered. On his twentieth birthday, I gifted him a bike. He was so happy and in turn, we were so happy for him."

The girl was getting interested. She sat up and focused her faculty on the soft whisper of the confessor.

"Then one day his principal called up to inform me that the cops had arrested him. I could not believe that the cops could arrest such a good boy. I rushed to Mumbai. At the police station I was told that he was arrested for raping and killing a girl. The whole world swirled and tumbled around me. I could not believe that my son could rape and kill. I met him and he just held my hand and wept like a baby. I wept too. I was committed to save my son. After all, as his father it was my duty to save him. I knew that I had given him the right set of values and that he could never commit such heinous crimes. I comforted him and called up a couple of my friends to engage a lawyer. I had made up my mind that I would save him.

While I was there at the police station, the police officer who was the case-incharge came and took me to his office. In his office, he introduced me to an elderly couple. When I was introduced to them, the lady grabbed me by my collar and slapped me. I was too shocked to react. After slapping me, she slumped on the chair and cried. Her husband consoled her. The case-incharge told me that they were the parents of the girl who was gang raped and then murdered by my son and his friends. He also told me that prima facie evidence went against my son and his friends. If that was not enough, he said that after raping and brutally murdering her—using rods to crack her skull, they doused her body with petrol taken from the bike of my son, to burn her body so that no one could recognize her. I was horrified. But the father in me still did not believe him.

I went ahead and hired the best lawyer. I had to sell off my shack. During this period I had no work to do but shuttle between Goa and Mumbai. People laughed at me, made fun of my wife and me, accused me of spoiling my son and what not. The case proceeded and the DNA report came from Hyderabad. Till that time I had some hope that the report would prove that my son was not involved. But the traces of semen, hair etc., proved that he was also a part of the gang that had raped and killed the girl. I went to see the lawyer. That day was the first day, when he said that my son was involved in the crime. But he assured me that being his lawyer, he would find ways and means to build a case and create doubt in the mind of the judge so that the term of my son could be reduced.

I got up and walked away, never to return to the lawyer or my son. The lawyer kept on calling me, asking for his fees but I never responded. I was shattered beyond repair. My only son being a rapist and a murderer? What sin did I commit to get such a son? I kept on following the case through newspapers and then one day the judge declared them guilty. Terming the case as rarest of rare, he pronounced death penalty for all the four accused. There was a lot of media hue and cry. Channels hounded me to have my byte, to invite me to panel discussions, to have my side of the story. But I shunned the entire world. My wife retracted into her shell and became a living corpse."

There was silence.

"One day I got a call from the jail authorities, stating that my son wanted to meet me for the last time before he was hanged. That night was the longest one in my life. I would have died every single second. My dreams, hopes, all were about to be wiped out forever. The only source of my joy would not be with me anymore. I cried through the night, seeking some solace but there was none. My wife just sat in the chair and the stream of tears from her eyes would not cease. She didn't say anything. There was no divinity coming our way. It seemed that Jesus had turned away his face from us. I knew he would be angry, as it was our son who had disgraced Him more than anyone.

I decided not to go and meet him. I did not want to be a part of the act he had committed. Though a part of me— the father, kept on goading me to go and see him. But for some reason I did not, rather I could not.

It has been more than a month since I buried his body. Sitting by his body, caressing his head and hair, I must have wept for hours. At that point in time I had just one wish. I wanted him to get up, look at me and call me Dad. My ears ached to hear his sweet voice.

Today, I confess that I feel guilty for not going to see him for the last time. He was a sinner, he had committed a terrible crime, but he was my son too. I let the law take its own course, but I should have let the father in me take his course too. I should have been there for him when he needed me the most. I deserted him. Why? Maybe I was too scared of my own value system, this church, Jesus and everyone? Maybe I could not figure out what was right and what was wrong and therefore mixed rights and duties. How could I have left my son, there in the jail, to wait for the day when he would be hung? I failed him as a father. True, he failed me as a son too. But then, aren't we both the same? Cowards and sinners! How different am I from him? He failed in his duties and so did I."

The girl wiped her tears silently. Till few minutes back she had no clue how a father thought and reacted. So involved was she in her own life that she could never figure out the point of view of her parents. An abyss grew inside her. She could not fathom the depth of the guilt pang, which hit her. How would her parents feel if she ended her life? If this man was ready to take his son back, despite being a rapist and a killer, won't her parents take her back, support and love her despite the fact that she was pregnant? They would shout, scream, cry, even curse her, the way this confessor did. But at the end of the day they would take her back. After all she was their only daughter. They wouldn't let a faulty decision of hers ruin the bond between them.

She felt the urge to throw open the confession box and run to her parents. She knew that just a sincere apology with tears, and an honest confession would set everything right.

She knew they would set things right for her, like always. She knew that all she had to do was reach out to them and everything would get sorted.

Dabbing her tears she sat there, motionless; deliberating. Was her situation as hopeless as she thought it to be? Was she right in assuming that there was no way out of it? Was she being fair to her parents when all they had for her was love?

There was a knock at the box. Through the little vents she could see a young man sitting. She looked at her watch, another forty minutes to go. She just wanted to be home, with her parents.

"Father, I have come here to confess that I have done something which will ensure that I burn in the fire of hell. I could never be a good son, a good brother. Now I have proved that I could not be a good husband too. I never had a very cordial relationship with my parents. For some reason, I was hell bent on doing exactly the opposite of what I was asked to do. It made me feel like a king, a rebel. It gave me a high. Though, in hindsight, I feel like a fool.

Much against their wishes, I married a girl. The reason they did not want me to get married was that I was not well-settled in life. But then I thought I was in love and like any other man, thought of marriage to be the culmination point. To prove a point, I walked out of my house and started living with my wife. It was only then that I realized how tough it was to run a household. Right from getting milk to making breakfast, cleaning, mopping, doing the dishes, buying groceries. I never knew how my mom managed all of this single-handedly.

In no time, love was made the sacrificial lamb. As my salary was not enough to take care of the household expenses, my wife had to step out to work. With the double income there was some respite from the mounting bills. But the long hours at work and household chores made her cranky and very snappy. I assumed that it would pass. Then one day she declared that she was pregnant. How could she get pregnant? I always used precaution. I was not ready to believe. Our lives had just started settling down, we had started saving some money. I knew that her pregnancy would ruin everything.

More than the joy of being an expectant father, my mind was clouded with the financial setback. No wonder, my wife was shocked to see my reaction. She asked me if I was not happy. Just to avoid any scene I lied and told her that I was. But the truth was that I felt like slapping her. I did not want a life where I had to work all my life to run my family, my house. I wanted to have some life of my own too.

After a few days, on a Sunday morning, I sat with her and presented her with the entire picture. I tried my best to convince her that we were not ready for a baby. I was being logical. It was not that I did not want a baby, but I definitely did not want it then. She threw a fit and told me that she was not ready to abort. We had a long argument. I went back to my parents' place. Of course they were worried. I did not tell them anything. My wife called me and asked me to come back." He started to sob.

"She told me that she would abort the baby as she loved me more than anything, more than her baby too. I felt horrible. I wanted to kiss her and tell her that she could keep the baby. But don't know why, I didn't. My scheming mind told me that before she could change her mind, I should get the abortion done. The very next day, I took her to a clinic. In a week or so, she recovered. But in reality, I think she never did. She just went numb, leading her life like a robot. Now she goes to work, earns her salary cheque, runs the household, but the woman in her is dead. The exuberant girl I fell in love with, is gone. And it is me who is responsible for two deaths; my baby and my beloved."

The girl in the confession box squirmed, her face streaked with tears.

"Was I such a weakling that I could not even afford to bring up my own kid? Why this apprehension? What were my insecurities? People long to have babies, go all the way to get one, and here I was, blessed by the Lord. Yet I decided to go against His wish. I know the Lord will never forgive me. And He has not. I am glad that He has punished me. Now that we are trying to conceive, she can't. Her doctor says that there is some complication with her fallopian tubes. Father, can you see the dichotomy? When I was blessed, I refused;

when I seek, I am being refused. I confess that I have failed my wife, my parents and even the Lord. I seek forgiveness. May the kind Lord forgive me for all my sins."

She was too stunned to react and sat there like a log while the sound of the man's footsteps faded. A feeling of repulsion spread over her. How could she be so self-centred? Why couldn't she make her boyfriend see the point of view shared by the man a few minutes back? Why did she hate her boyfriend? Maybe he was too naïve to realize the true worth of the situation and to appreciate the goodness of life and the Lord's blessing. Maybe, with time he would turn out to be a good father, a good husband. How could she hate the same man whom she had loved for his intellect, charm and a million other things? If all those qualities were still there, then what was the reason to hate him?

She looked at her watch. Her time was up. She just wanted to run back home, to the warm embrace of her mom, tearing the suicide note and getting ready to face the consequences. After all, someone had to face them, so why not her?

***

"Oh Lord, forgive me for lying to the girl that I had some important work to attend to. May your light guide her and protect her. Amen." The Father lit a candle.

ભ❖ৡ

Writer's Block

It was a middle-class apartment complex. The stairway was dimly lit. Though there were two elevators, but for reasons only known to him, he took the stairs. Wearing a bottle green shirt, trousers and a cap, he was carrying a big messenger bag. He stopped at the fourth floor and looked around. There were four apartments; two on each side. 401, 402, 403, 404. He read the number plates. In a state of quandary, he stood there, weighing the pros and cons. As if he figured it out, he quickly walked towards the staircase and took the flight of stairs towards the fifth floor landing. Suddenly, he stopped and turned around. In no time he started descending the stairs.

He stood before the door of apartment 404 and adjusted the strap of his messenger bag, which was slung across his right shoulder. He took a deep breath and pressed the doorbell. As he waited, he strained his ears to pick any sound at the other side of the door.

"Yes?" The door slowly creaked with the chain-lock in place.

"Sorry Sir, for coming so late. But there is an urgent courier for you."

"Courier at eleven in the night? The guard did not stop you?" The apartment owner's reaction was justified.

Impervious to his reaction, the courier guy opened his bag and pulled out a medium sized packet. It was neatly wrapped in bamboo paper. With a click, the man on the other side of the door unlocked the chain and the door swung open on its hinges.

"Who has sent it?" The apartment owner enquired.

"Sir, it is from Baroda." The courier guy answered.

"Let me get my glasses. Can't read much without them." The apartment owner walked inside.

The courier guy waited for a second, looked around and also got inside the apartment. In no time, he bolted the door from inside and quickly scanned the set-up. It was a middle-class apartment. The living area had a conventional maroon sofa set, with dark, oily patches near the headrest. The coffee table seemed to have come in dowry. The dining area also had a dowry gift; a dining table with four chairs. The table was loaded with an assortment of ketchup and pickle bottles, a coaster set, glasses and a spoon holder.

There were two crooked abstract paintings and in the twin light holder, one bulb was fused. The curtains needed dry cleaning on an urgent basis. One side of the room had a bar, which was open, and on the counter, a glass and a whiskey bottle were placed.

"What are you doing inside?" The apartment owner walked out from one of the rooms and for obvious reason was shocked to see the courier guy standing inside his apartment. "Give me the packet and please leave." The owner, in his late forties, dressed in a track bottom and tee was clearly agitated.

The courier guy smiled.

"I will complain against this outrageous behavior of yours. Don't blame me if you get fired." The tone had more fear than threat.

The courier guy still had the smile stuck to his face.

"Before I call the cops, give me the packet and get lost."

The insulting tone did not go well with the courier guy as his facial muscles twitched. He put his hand inside the bag. In no time, he flicked out a revolver and aimed it at the apartment owner.

"The cops will come for sure, but only to find your body lying here, on the floor, amidst a pool of blood. You want that?" The revolver waved just a few feet from the owner. It caused fear and panic all over his face.

The courier guy removed the bag from his shoulder and put it on the floor. "You make any noise and I won't hesitate to shoot you. I hope you can see the silencer fitted on the barrel."

"What is this? Who are you?" The owner was hit by a bolt of lightning and was having difficulty in finding words.

"For sure not your next door, friendly courier guy." He gave out a throaty laugh.

"Move back, just two steps, and sit down on the dining chair. Very slowly and without making any sudden movement."

"Listen, you have got the wrong guy." The apartment owner clarified.

"On my word, one and two." The instructions were clear.

The apartment owner failed to respond.

The courier guy moved towards him and cracked a sharp slap on his face. Owing to the brutal force, the man fell on the chair.

"Just keep your mouth shut or the next time there will be a bullet hitting you instead of my hand."

The courier guy pulled out a rope from his bag and secured the apartment owner; his hands tied to his back and his feet to the legs of the chair.

"I am sure you know why I haven't tied your mouth." The courier guy whispered in his ear. Horror and fear were written clearly on the face of the owner.

"Just tell me where is the key to your wardrobe and what all worthwhile you have in the apartment. Better be quick and this ordeal will get over in no time."

"Seriously, you have got the wrong guy. There is not much in here, just household goods." A tear trickled down the face of the apartment owner. The earlier slap had made his left cheek turn red. Maybe the courier guy suffered from Obsessive Compulsive Disorder and could not see the other cheek without any red color. He slapped him again, turning the other cheek red too, and curing his OCD temporarily.

"I am not here to waste time, quick with the keys."

The apartment owner now started to sob.

"Now you sit here quietly and I shall do the needful."

He walked inside the apartment. It was a two-room apartment. The first room, which had an adjoining washroom, was probably his bedroom. There was a double bed with a side table and a wardrobe. The other room, surprisingly, had wall-to-wall bookshelves. The shelves were crammed with books. Religion, fiction, politics and biographies. Every possible genre was there.

"So you are into reading?" He called out as his eyes scanned the wall-to-wall bookshelves.

"Yes, that is my job." His voice had a strange mix of sullen fear and fatigue.

The courier guy came out of the room and walked towards the bar. He peered inside expectantly, "What kind of job are you into?"

"I am a publisher."

"Interesting!" He came out of the room and sat across the dining table, looking towards the bar.

"I guess, not a successful one as I can't see any single malt in here."

"Well, you can say that. Listen, I don't have anything which might interest you. I really don't have anything to offer," he pleaded.

"So what stopped you from being a successful one?" The question was sardonic.

"That is one long story." His face still had fear written all over it. "Please take whatever you want and leave. I don't deserve to die."

"Just because I'm having a conversation, don't assume even for a moment that I can't kill you. And I can't leave right now due to two reasons. One, I'm cursing myself for walking into your apartment when I could have gone into any other, made my day and left. Here, all I can see is books and books and more books. The second reason is that the cops are most active at this hour. They stop every car, every bike, even every auto rickshaw. So, I will leave around five am, when the streets are empty."

"You are intelligent for the kind of work you do." The cynicism was evident.

"Who told you that the work I do does not involve intelligence?" He countered. "Picking the right home, the right target, the right day, the right time, everything requires a high level of intelligence. Just one slip and the game ends. Unlike publishing, in my trade there are no second chances."

The contempt insulted the publisher. "Listen, you have seen the house; please take whatever catches your fancy but please don't comment on things you don't even know about."

"And what makes you think that my only expertise is burglary?"

"You don't have any expertise there too. It is evident. Look, what kind of house you have chosen. Not a thing in sight. Had you been good at your job you would have done precise prospecting and chosen a rich man's place. And do you think I would expect a burglar to know about publishing? Even if he is an intelligent one?" Some more acerbity was served by the publisher.

In a flash of a second, the courier guy moved towards the publisher and pressed his revolver against his forehead. In a fit of rage, he cocked the hammer. "You bastard, who has given you the right to scoff at everyone? What the fuck do you know about anything? I am so tempted to blow your brains off. But then just the thought that you won't be worth all the pain stops me."

"I am sorry, I really am." The plead was feeble and delivered in a shaky tone.

"Like everyone, you also understand the language of fear. I have been trying to be considerate with you, but the moment you see me getting a little soft, you start taking advantage." He released the hammer.

"I am sorry."

"Shut up. You don't mean it when you say you are sorry. You are just afraid. Shit scared to die. Aren't you?" He cocked the hammer again. "Tell me, did you mean it when you said sorry? Were you really sorry? Speak the truth or else I shall pull the trigger."

The publisher started shivering like a leaf, "I am sorry, now I am, I wasn't sorry earlier, now I am. I am really sorry." He stuttered, "Please don't kill me. Please."

"I hate you guys. If you guys were not so despicable, I would not have been here."

The publisher was still shivering.

"People like you forced me to take this path." The statement was not addressed to the publisher, it was mumbled and directed at no one in particular.

"I am sorry."

"Shut up. Why can't you stop apologizing?"

"I mean I am sorry for what they did to you."

"And how would that help me?" He still had the barrel pressed to the publisher's forehead.

"Maybe I can set it right." His eyes oscillated between the barrel and the face of the courier guy.

"Are you even aware what wrong was committed and by whom?"

"I could be wrong but I guess some publishers rejected

your work which forced you to become a burglar."

"You are not as dumb as you sound." He laughed. "And Sir, how can you set it right?" The cold sarcasm was very measured.

"Maybe I can publish your work." A path of truce was proposed.

"With a gun to your head?" His laughter sounded very eerie in the entire scheme of things.

The publisher decided to remain silent. He looked at the courier guy. "See, I have nothing to lose as I'm a loser right now too. My wife left me long back as she thought I was crazy to be a publisher who was concerned about the literary content of the script rather than its marketability. She found someone else to cater to her demands. Fortunately we never had a child, as she could not conceive one. Wanted to go for IVF or some other way, but the treatment was too expensive. I have shifted seven offices in the last nine years. Now this apartment serves as my office too. Credit card goons have started coming over to my place on a daily basis. But then I don't have any money. It would have been so much better if in a fit of rage you had killed me. But yes, for some reason, after going through all this humiliation, I was afraid to die. Don't know why. I mean what do I have to hold on to? Why was I shivering? What was holding me back? Who will cry if I'm gone? Yes, you were right when you said that I am not worth the pain of killing. The cops, the municipality, everyone would have cursed me when they would have come to take away my decaying body."

The courier guy got up and inspected the bar. He pulled out two glasses and poured Blender's Pride into them. While he did, his eyes were focused on the trickle of the whiskey falling into the glass.

Holding both the glasses, he walked towards the publisher, and put the glass to his lips. "Take a large sip. I would have added some ice to it but it seems your refrigerator is not working. The bread inside has got fungus thicker than the slice itself." He complained

The publisher took a large sip. "I don't cook anymore. Either I eat out or order something." A drop of whiskey trickled from the side of his mouth, finding its way to his neck.

The courier guy did bottoms up and banged the glass on the table. The rush of the bitter warmth, which hit his senses, made him cringe his face for a split second.

"You know there is something common and something not so common between us." He sat there, looking at the face of the clock. "We both are losers, in our own ways, but I gave up, ending up as a bigger loser; and you are still fighting. So you are not a loser, but a fighter. Yes, you are a fighter." The courier guy walked towards him, holding the glass and letting him have another sip.

"You know, I did my English literature from Presidency College, Kolkata. With literature lovers in my family, I aspired being a writer. Spent two years or maybe more completing my first manuscript. I was sure that it would get me a Booker, if not the Nobel Prize." He looked at the publisher. "I know I was being naïve. But I really wanted to be famous. I sent across my manuscript over e-mail first, to top rankers. Never got any reply. Then to the second rung publishing houses; again no response. Then I started going personally, yet no response. Then was forced to gatecrash. It took me more than three years, I covered every single publisher, but no one, not even one showed any interest in my work. They thought that it was verbose, out of context and not fit for consumption."

He walked towards the publisher and put the glass to his lips and this time forced the remaining liquid down his throat. The publisher coughed.

"It will burn a little but will settle down."

He then walked towards the bar and poured himself another large one.

"Don't worry, I will pay for these drinks. Can't leave you with an empty bar." He smiled.

"You know why my work was not fit for consumption?" He was all worked up.

"Because people are used to trash. Serve a pig a plate of black forest cake and some shit and we know what would go its way. We have turned literature into a cesspool of mediocrity, PR and marketing game and a hiding place for losers. Writers have become salesmen, selling themselves at every opportunity, shamelessly asking people to buy, to read. Where is the dignity part? Is literature all about selling?"

"I can understand your plight." The publisher tried consoling him.

"No, you can't."

"Yes, I can, as I have faced the same." The publisher explained. "I could not change my thinking and see where I am. Can't even get the compressor of my refrigerator fixed. Can I have another drink?"

He walked towards him and looked into his eyes. "Can I trust you?"

"Well, we are on different sides of the table. You shouldn't." The publisher was honest.

"The side is the same, the loser's side."

"But you just said that you were a loser whereas I was the fighter."

"Nevertheless a loser, a fighter who lost."

"Think before you act."

"Thinking is a waste of time."

"Losers have plenty of it." The publisher tried setting the context.

"What good is abundance if it has no value?"

"Time decides the value."

"So why has it not till now?" The courier guy seemed agitated.

"Maybe the time was not right."

"What makes you think now it is?"

"Time brought us here. And only time knows the outcome."

"What does it want us to do?"

"Respect time, and do our bit."

"We have being doing our bit for so long."

"Time was not right."

"What is the guarantee that it is right now?"

"To know, we have to do our bit, again."

"What is your bit?"

"To read your script less any prejudice and bias."

"And mine?"

"To hand me your manuscript, less any apprehension or bias."

"What if you reject it?"

"You still get to walk away with whatever you have in the gunny bag."

"And if you like it?"

"I will publish it and will do my best to sell it. Even then, you get to walk away with whatever you have stuffed in the gunny bag."

"Do you hate me?"

"It is all contextual."

"Do you think I will fall for your trap and open your hands?"

"We have to do our bit."

***

They were seated in the room with wall-to-wall bookshelves. The publisher was sitting at his workstation, with the tall lamp on, reading the manuscript intently, which was given to him by the courier guy. Like the love of his life, he always carried it with him.

"Could you pour me another drink?" The publisher requested.

The courier guy looked at him and smiled, "It seems that the sides of the table have changed."

"It is good to keep changing to remain current, and yes... could you get me another refill please? I have just another thirty pages to go."

***

"How do you like it?"

"It is the end that decides the fate of any story." The publisher looked up.

"You mean the beginning is of no consequence?"

"What good is any beginning if it fails to lead to a logical conclusion. My drink please."

"Check out the bar. There would be a bottle of Absolut stacked somewhere. Get that."

"But why to mix our drinks?"

"Are you afraid?"

"Do you think I should be?"

"Answer me, are you?"

"What do you think?"

"My thinking has nothing to do with the fact. Are you?"

"God, you are obstinate."

"And you are brilliant."

"Shut up."

"No, I mean it."

"What?"

"You poser, as if you didn't get it."

"No, I didn't."

"I love your work and will publish it. Maybe this is the dream script, which I have been waiting for. You got yourself a deal."

"Really?"

"Get that vodka first."

"You really mean you will publish it?"

"But I don't have any advance to pay."

"Would it sell?

"Let us do our bit."

"Wow. What do we do now?"

"Could you get the vodka please?"

"What do we call it?"

"Mmm... maybe Café Latte."

ଓ✣ଈ

Glossary

Aloo Paratha	An Indian recipe and one of the most popular breakfast dishes throughout western, central and northern regions of India
Aloo-gobhi	A famous vegetable preparation from India, which uses Potato and Cauliflower.
Amma	Mother
Baba	Father
Bhaiya	Brother
Beta	Son
Bidda Balan	A famous Bollywood actress
Baniya	People hailing from the business community

Behanji	Sister
Bharat mata ki jai	A war cry used by Indian armed forces
Chacha	Uncle
Chapati	Indian bread
Chane-bhature	A heavy north Indian meal comprising spicy chick peas and deep fried white flour bread.
Chaar	Number four
Dada	Elder brother
Dal	Lentil cooked with water, turmeric and salt
Dupatta	A piece of cloth worn to cover head or chest by women of northern and central India
Dainik Jagran	A Hindi newspaper
Gora Sahib	A British officer
Guru	A teacher
Gurumaa	A teacher worthy of being a mother
Jaan	Darling
Jawaan	Young man
Ji	A suffix added after name as a mark of respect
Janaab	Sir
Jija	Brother in law

Maa	Mother
Paapu	Father
Paanch	Number five
Ram Ram	A common way of greeting people in the northern part of India
Roti	Indian flat bread
Salwar-suit	Long shirt worn with loose pants by women of north India.
Saree	Traditional Indian six-yard long drape for women
Saas-bahu	Mother-in-law and daughter-in-law
Sahib	Master
Saale	An Indian abuse used in day-to-day conversation

www.ingramcontent.com/pod-product-compliance
Lightning Source LLC
Chambersburg PA
CBHW031232260626
47169CB00007B/2260